COPING WITH

Cross-Cultural and Interracial Relationships

Sandra Lee Smith

THE ROSEN PUBLISHING GROUP, INC./NEW YORK

Published in 1990 by The Rosen Publishing Group, Inc.
29 East 21st Street, New York, NY 10010

First Edition

Manufactured in the United States of America

Library of Congress Cataloging-In-Publication Data

Smith, Sandra Lee.
Coping with cross-cultural and interracial relationships / Sandra Lee Smith.—1st ed.
p. cm.
Includes bibliographical references.
Summary: Describes how to relate to people of other cultures, races, and religions, discussing such areas as language, cultural heritage, discrimination, and attitude.
ISBN 0-8239-1157-8
1. Ethnic groups—Cross-cultural studies—Juvenile literature. 2. Interpersonal relations—Juvenile literature. 3. Discrimination—United States—Juvenile literature. 4. United States—Ethnic relations—Juvenile literature. [1. Ethnic groups. 2. Ethnic relations.] I. Title.
GN495.4.S65 1990
305.8—dc20 69-77303
CIP
AC

To my teenage nephew John Prendergast,
my teenage niece Karen Prendergast
and my teenage nephew Michael Prendergast,
a special wish for positive and successful interaction
and relationships in the years to come.

ABOUT THE AUTHOR ◇

For twenty-one years, Sandra Lee Smith has taught grades from kindergarten through college level in California and Arizona. Her extensive travels in Canada and Central and South America have included observations in public and private schools as well as teacher training programs.

As a consultant in connection with Arizona State University, where she obtained her M.A. in Bilingual/Multicultural Education, she has conducted workshops for teachers and parents throughout the Southwest.

Ms. Smith has been hired as a consultant by the Central Valley Teacher Education Center in California and the Bureau of Indian Affairs in New Mexico to teach aspects of the whole language process.

Active on legislative committees and in community projects, she has helped design programs to involve parents in the education process.

In response to the President's Report, *A Nation at Risk*, Ms. Smith participated in a project involving Arizona State University, Phoenix Elementary School District, and an inner-city community in Phoenix. Participants in the project developed a holistic approach to education that Ms. Smith and others successfully implemented in their classrooms; from their research and application, a whole language program emerged involving the three C's—Composition, Comprehension, and Critical Thinking.

Contents

	Introduction	1
1	Coping with Cultural Differences	5
2	Coping with Different Languages	18
3	Coping with Different Faiths	33
4	Coping Across Economic Classes	44
5	Overcoming Prejudice	58
6	Envy and Fear Destroy	71
7	What an Act of Kindness Can Do	86
8	How Patience Affects Interaction	101
9	Your Attitude Makes A Difference	115
10	What Goes Around Comes Around	129
	Recommended Reading	141
	Index	143

Introduction

The United States has been called a "melting pot," and indeed we are a blend of peoples from many cultures. Our history shows a steady movement of immigrants, and they are still pouring in. America offers hope, freedom, and opportunity. Men, women, and children flock to it to find jobs, seek education, and live what they hope will be a better life.

People come from every country on the globe. Some periods of time reflect large numbers from one country. For example, during the Hungarian revolution, a large number of Hungarians arrived. When the war in Vietnam ended, thousands of Vietnamese immigrated.

These people bring their own language, religion, and culture. Often they seem strange to us; it is difficult to understand their speech, their ways, and even the clothes they wear.

The freedom in America encourages these people to leave their homes and come to this country. We take for granted the many opportunities we enjoy. Most of us can decide what jobs we want to pursue. If it turns out that we don't like that job, or if we want something different later in life, we have the freedom to seek, train, and apply for other work.

That may not sound like a big deal, but in many countries teenagers are forced to take over the businesses run by their parents. What do your mother and father do? Would you want to have the same work? Maybe so. But if not, in America you can decide to seek a different career.

In school, students in this country can decide what courses to take. In some countries teenagers cannot even go to school. Often, they come to the United States so that they can receive an education. Imagine not knowing how to read or write. We take those skills for granted, but they give us freedom to seek whatever opportunity we desire.

In this country we have freedom to worship in whatever manner we choose. Religion is an important part of most cultures. The fact that people can bring their religion and beliefs with them to this country gives them the courage to make the move.

Because of these freedoms and opportunities, we have ended up with a mixture of races, cultures, and languages. Some people have difficulty adjusting. Perhaps they don't understand a group of people different from themselves. Or perhaps they are afraid they themselves will have to make unwanted changes.

When new cultures arrive and become integrated into our society, change does occur. Change is never an easy process, especially if you are not the one choosing to make it. Some people view change as a threat; they may lose some of their confidence or security. Some people don't want old traditions to disappear because it becomes easier for new ones to take over.

Most people, however, view this change and blend of new peoples as healthy. When there are mixtures of languages and cultures, things are viewed differently. New ideas develop. Tolerance grows. Life does not become static or boring.

Anyone who can speak more than one language can tell you how enlightening that is. Our thoughts are controlled by our language. If you know more than one language, you have more ways of looking at a problem, an event, or life in general. It broadens a person's view and increases brain power.

In spite of the long-range positive effects of multicultural interaction, problems exist in dealing with the immediate reality. You are going through many adjustments in the process of moving from child to adult. The last thing you need or want are more changes, yet they are there.

Everytime you interact with someone or establish a relationship, it can cause you to make some changes. Because our society is so diverse, the likelihood of meeting people from another culture, faith, social class, or race is extremely high. We can learn to cope with it and make it a positive experience.

The most obvious clash of cultures occurs when an American must interact with someone who has just arrived from a foreign country. The language differences alone can create a difficult situation. To further compound the problem, there may be racial differences as well.

Religion is ingrained in a culture, and people rarely change their views. Because religious freedom is part of the American Constitution, Americans need to learn to interact with friends and acquaintances who are of different faiths.

Another cultural difference in our society is more subtle. Economic background creates different life-styles and values. In some countries teens are not allowed to mingle with teens from other social classes. For example, a wealthy student would never be allowed to attend a school with needy students. That is not the case in America.

Our public schools have students from all economic backgrounds, attending the same classes, playing on the same sport teams, and belonging to the same clubs and organizations. Deep friendships often develop across class lines. It may be difficult for students to cope with friends who have more or less money than they do, but on the whole, this social mobility is healthy for America.

In this book, we shall look at the variety of cultures that exists today in the United States and at techniques for coping. It is healthy for a country to be multicultural, and since America has a varied society, it is important to learn how to cope with it.

CHAPTER ◇ 1

Coping with Cultural Differences

The United States is a large country, spanning a continent east to west, crossing an ocean and extending north to Alaska. It is true that American culture is mixed. Some of the differences are simply regional. For example, life-styles in New York, the Florida Keys, the Pacific Northwest, and the Hawaiian Islands are not exactly the same.

Some of the regional differences are the result of climate. Teenagers in Alaska spend their winter weekends differently than teenagers in Arizona. Long winter nights and cold weather keep teens indoors in the northern state; sunny days and temperate weather allow Southwesterners to be outdoors most of the winter. The difference in activities is obvious. Some ski regularly and others have never even seen snow.

Another factor in cultural differences is geographical variations. The surfers on the California coast would not be a subcultural group in North Dakota, where there are no ocean waves. Yet you will probably find a similar subculture in Hawaii, even though it is several thousand miles distant.

Another geographical factor is the national borders. Towns along the U.S./Mexico border have a different subculture than those along the U.S./Canada border. Along the Canadian border, you will find one subculture near French Canada and another in English Canada. Hawaii has a mixture of Japanese and Pacific Island cultures because of its location.

In spite of the differences across our country, an amazing number of similarities exist. If you travel from Washington, D.C. to San Francisco, you will see many of the same chains of stores, restaurants, and gas stations. The same television networks broadcast nationwide, and on the radio similar music is played across the land.

English is spoken in most places. Other languages may be spoken within a cultural group. For example, the Navajo in Arizona are Americans who speak another language. The basic language of business, schools, and entertainment, however, is English.

In contrast, look at a map of Europe and travel the same distance across that continent. How many countries did you go through? What languages did you encounter? You would not find the same chains of stores, restaurants, and gas stations across the miles and borders.

European teens are used to dealing with multicultural differences. In school, they learn several languages. This is practical for them because they will need to use the languages. Different life-styles pose little threat because everyone grows up knowing those differences, and they need not change your life.

In the United States the situation is different. Americans

expect to find similarities when they travel because that is what *they* are used to. This very expectation is what makes it difficult for many Americans to travel to foreign countries. They usually don't find life the same as at home.

In most small towns and in the majority of the United States, Americans are not used to facing people from different countries. Some of the larger high schools have exchange programs and bring in a handful of foreign students. Very few students, however, have a chance to interact with them.

Americans who live in large cities where immigrants enter the United States and those who live along a border have an advantage over the average American in dealing with multicultural differences. They are exposed to other cultures and learn from an early age that there are differences and similarities.

Since students in the city are more likely to encounter cultural differences, lets look at Carla and Jaime, who are students at North High School.

Carla and her brother Jaime entered the hallway of the high school building. As they passed the office, the door opened and Mrs. Ruiz, one of the secretaries, stepped out. Spotting Carla and Jaime, she waved for them to join her.

"Oh, no," Carla muttered under her breath. "I hope it isn't more new students."

Jaime, always trying to be positive, said, "Maybe she wants us to take messages. We'll get out of first-period class."

Carla gave him one of her looks that said, "Get real."

As she entered the office and saw the people standing at the counter, Carla knew she had been right. Her heart sank when she spotted the girl half hiding behind her father. One look at her starched white blouse, uniform skirt, and worn-out flats and Carla wanted to turn around and march right out.

She didn't, of course. Mrs. Ruiz had taken her arm and was propelling her toward the counter to meet the new student.

"Carla, this is Maria Garcia. She and her brother are from . . ."

Mexico. Carla didn't need to be told. Lots of people were arriving from there; more and more each day. She knew why. Jobs. Opportunity. All that freedom hype. Grandpapa had told her at least a hundred times why he had come from Sonora to the "mighty land of opportunity."

Because her grandparents had come from Mexico, Carla and Jaime knew a little Spanish. It wasn't fair. Just because they spoke the language, they were always getting stuck taking the new students around.

Carla sighed with frustration while Mrs. Ruiz introduced Jaime to Juan Garcia. At least Juan didn't look too different. His purple shirt was obviously made in Mexico, but other than that he looked much like Jaime. Maybe that was why her brother never minded showing new kids around. The boys never looked too out of it.

Maria, on the other hand, was obviously not going to blend in. Nobody wore a uniform at North High. Those awful flats were way out. And her hair. Maria definitely needed to style that straight cut.

When Jaime and Juan left, Mrs. Ruiz propelled Carla toward Maria. Maria slipped behind her father. For goodness sake, Carla thought, I'm not going to bite. That was another area where Jaime lucked out. The girls were always scared.

With a sigh and a resolve to be patient, Carla motioned

for Maria to follow. "*Venga*. Come with me. I'll show you your classes."

Maria hesitated. Her father murmured to her in Spanish until finally she peered around him at Carla.

Suddenly Carla felt ashamed of being annoyed. The girl must have sensed it and didn't want to go with her. Too bad she had to, Carla thought, and then forced a smile.

"*Esta bien*," she continued in her accented Spanish. "You'll like our school. There are some really cute guys in our sophomore class."

Maria smiled at that, and Carla felt a little better herself. Before she could get annoyed again, she turned and headed out the door, motioning for Maria to follow. Out of the corner of her vision she saw Mrs. Ruiz give Maria a polite push on her way. Carla sighed.

In the hall it took only a few open stares at Maria to embarrass Carla. For the third time, Carla asked herself why she always had to be the one to do this. Maybe if she walked a little faster, nobody would know she was with the Mexican student.

"Carla," someone called from the hall. "Wait up."

Carla glanced around and saw Sally waving at her. Carla's shoulders slumped when she recognized the most popular girl in the sophomore class. What was she going to think of Maria?

Sally's blonde curls swung across her shoulders as she worked her way through the crowded hall. When she got to Carla she smiled and then nodded to Maria.

"Another new student?" she asked.

Carla rolled her eyes and gave a persevering sigh. "This is Maria."

To her surprise, Sally smiled at Maria and spoke in heavily accented Spanish. "*Buenos dias*."

Maria muttered some response, but she was obviously tongue-tied.

"I'm learning Spanish," Sally beamed, quite proud of herself.

Carla stared. "What for?" she asked.

"So I can talk to the new students. Why d'you think?"

Carla was too stunned to answer. The second bell rang, and she knew she'd have to hurry Maria through the crowd. Luckily, her first class was the same as Maria's.

"We have to get to class," Carla explained as she waved good-bye to Sally. "See you at lunch."

And, she thought, she'd make sure Maria was nowhere in sight.

Maria sat through first-period class looking terrified. The teacher spoke in English, and it sounded like gibberish to her. How was she going to pass her classes when she couldn't understand a word? Not only that, the American girl, Carla, hated her. Sure, she acted all right and showed her the class and where to sit, but Maria could tell that Carla did not want to help her.

Maria glanced down at her clothes. Last night she had been so excited. *Mama* had helped her iron her best blouse, and Juan had polished her shoes. But it had done no good. Everyone stared as if she were a clown. She wanted to run home now and never come back.

A tear started to form but Maria blinked it back. One of the boys was staring at her. She wouldn't let him see that she was afraid. She blinked again and sat very still.

The teacher continued to talk, but to Maria's horror no one was listening. Carla was passing notes to the girl across the aisle. The boys beside her were chewing pieces of paper and then throwing them across the room.

Maria waited for the teacher to slap their hands with a

ruler. The Sisters at the School of Santo Domingo would never let this happen. Students were expelled for less.

The teacher continued talking as if nothing were happening. Maria became concerned, wondering if the teacher was blind or maybe deaf. Students were whispering to each other, but none talked to Maria.

Maria wished she were back home in the small town of San Luis. She missed her friends. Instead of being embarrassed to be seen with her, Lupe and Carmen would walk with her to school. Every morning they would stop at the *panaderia* and buy a fresh roll still hot from the oven.

Not today and probably never again. Maria hadn't seen anything like a bakery. She had ridden on the bus down a four-lane highway. Cars and tall buildings were all she had seen. Not flowers. Not the old man who swept the streets. Not a smiling face anywhere.

The bell rang, and Maria sat up alarmed. Now what? Carla was scurrying out the door. She would have to hurry to catch up. A boy shoved her aside as she tried to get down the aisle of desks.

"Move it. Why don't you go back where you came from?"

Maria didn't understand all the words, but she recognized the tone. Her father had papers. They had stood in line at the consulate for weeks to get their permits. There was nothing to be afraid of, she reminded herself.

To her relief, Carla poked her head in the doorway and told her to hurry. Relieved that the American hadn't deserted her, Maria hurried past the frowning boy and pushed out of the room.

Carla waited with a bored expression and when she saw Maria motioned her to follow. She paused at the door to another classroom and pointed.

"This is your next class, Maria. I have to go to Geometry. Just have a seat. When the bell rings, go to your next class, which is across the hall."

Maria tried to calm the panic as she looked where Carla had pointed.

"After that class, it's lunch. If you don't see me, just follow everyone to the cafeteria. I'll find you before the bell rings."

Maria wanted to grab Carla and make her stay. She would have begged except that Carla gave her such a look of disgust.

For several seconds she stood outside the classroom watching Carla disappear down the hall. She wanted to run and hide. Those who passed by stared. No one smiled. Frantic and afraid, she searched the hall for Juan. If she saw her brother she would beg him to take her home.

No familiar face showed in the crowd. Thinking maybe it would be safer in the classroom, she finally opened the door and stepped inside. Several students were laughing, but as the door closed behind her, silence fell. Everyone stared. Maria wanted the floor to open up and swallow her. She blinked back a tear that threatened to fall.

"Maria," someone shouted from the back of the room.

To her surprise, she saw a blond American girl waving and pointing to an empty seat. It was Sally, and she was smiling.

The lunch bell rang, and Jaime hurried to Room 204. Juan would be in a panic if he didn't get there before class let out.

"Hey, Jaime, what's up?"

Jaime turned to see a couple of his buddies standing by

the lockers. For a brief second he was tempted to join them, but then he remembered Juan.

"Meet you outside," he hollered over the heads of passing students. "I've got to pick up someone."

Bodies seemed to merge into a wall, blocking his way. Jaime shouldered through the oncoming traffic and finally arrived at Room 204. The teacher had just dismissed class. Jaime sighed with relief. He'd made it.

"*Bueno*," Jaime called out as Juan came through the door. The way Juan's face creased in a smile made the mad dash worth the effort. Jaime knew how Juan must feel. He'd been a stranger in a foreign school before. It was enough to scare the life out of you.

The trip down the hall was easier this time since they went with the flow of traffic. As they walked, Jaime asked Juan about his classes. Their Spanish mingled in with the English that surrounded them.

"I don't know," Juan explained. "It is hard to understand the teacher. It's going to be tough."

"Don't worry," Jaime assured him. "You'll be surprised how fast you learn English. Besides, I'll be glad to help. You can come to my house to study anytime."

Before Juan had a chance to thank him, they caught up to Mark and Wayne. Jaime introduced Juan to his friends. He could tell that they didn't really want to bother getting to know a stranger, especially one who didn't speak English, but Jaime ignored their unspoken attitude. He continued to act as if Juan belonged. Every once in a while he would translate a funny comment or a joke so that Juan would feel included. It was no big deal to Jaime. He was glad to help.

Several feminine giggles carried across the courtyard. Jaime recognized Carla's. He glanced over at the group of girls and frowned. Maria was not with them.

"Wayne, my man, keep an eye on Juan for me. I'll be right back." After a quick assurance to Juan, Jaime slipped over to the group of sophomores and nudged his sister.

Her smile faded when she swung around to face Jaime's stern expression.

"Where's Maria?"

"I don't know," Carla said. "She was in a different class. I couldn't find her."

"And you aren't looking that hard either," he accused.

"Hey, come off it. I get tired having to baby-sit all these weirdos. If you're so worried, you go find her."

Jaime clenched his jaw, trying to prevent himself from saying something he'd regret. Too bad his younger sister hadn't gone to school in another country as he had. He could still remember walking into that classroom of Japanese students. He hadn't understood a word of their language, nor had any idea what he was supposed to do. His major memory was of monumental fear.

Carla wouldn't know about that. She had stayed home with Mama when his father had taken him along the year he'd worked abroad for his company. If there were only some way Jaime could make her understand.

"Go look for her, please." He tried to sweet-talk her. "Do it for me then."

"You're just as weird as they are," she accused and smiled when her friends giggled.

Jaime shook his head. As he turned away he spotted Maria. His throat tightened when he saw her standing alone and obviously ill at ease. He hurried to her side.

"Your brother is over here. Come with us."

Her smile of relief was catching. Jaime grinned and decided that Maria was actually a very pretty girl. He vowed then and there to show her around to her afternoon classes even if he had to be tardy for his own.

* * *

Think about the reactions of the students to Juan and Maria Garcia. If you have had foreign students in your school, you probably recognize some of the reactions. Perhaps you've felt the same way yourself.

Even if you have never encountered students from a foreign country, you might recognize the situation. Students often react the same way to any new student, American or foreign.

Let's look at Carla's reaction. Why do you suppose it was so negative? Carla did not want to help Maria. It may not necessarily be because she's mean or ill-mannered. If you look closely, Carla was worried about herself. She was *embarrassed* to be seen with Maria. Why is that?

When we encounter someone new or different or when we must associate with them, it creates stress. It seems silly to worry about what other people will think to see you with someone who is different, but it is a very real fear. People who are not sure of themselves or who lack confidence often worry too much about what other people think of them. Carla was so busy worrying about what her friends would say that she didn't have time to consider Maria's feelings.

Jamie was much more understanding. Why do you think that was so?

Jaime could empathize, or put himself in Juan's place. In fact, he had been in a similar situation himself, so he knew what fear Juan and Maria were suffering. He could identify with their feelings because he had had them himself.

Maria, we know, was definitely afraid. What reasons does she have to be afraid? Would you be fearful in her situation?

People look at someone who is different and have the idea that the person is what they see. We forget that inside, he or she is a mass of feelings that become tangled into all kinds of reactions. It takes compassion, such as Jaime's, to understand what new foreign students are experiencing.

Not everyone can be fortunate enough to travel to a foreign country, let alone attend school there. Carla's lack of experience obviously made it difficult for her to share Maria's feelings. But is that an excuse not to treat foreign students with kindness or assistance?

Sally had an interesting response to Maria. What do you think prompted that? Sally had never been to a foreign country. In fact, she had never been out of the city. Yet she had compassion for Maria's situation and eased it considerably by a simple hello and a smile.

Do you think Sally suffered by being friendly with Maria? She obviously wasn't worried about what her friends thought about associating with an immigrant from Mexico. She did take a risk that her friends might not like her anymore. Maybe friends like that lack confidence and self-assurance.

In reality, it is very unlikely that you will lose friends because you are nice to strangers. Jaime certainly wasn't worried about what his friends thought. Jaime was more worried about Juan and Maria. Jaime's friends didn't make a scene about Juan's joining them. If they were bothered at all, it was likely that they were like Carla, afraid of what people would think.

Fear is the major factor in dealing with strangers. Carla was afraid of what her friends were thinking. Maria was afraid because she didn't understand, and she was worried about what the students were thinking of her when they stared. Jaime was fearful that Juan and Maria were afraid.

Once fear is identified as the root of the problems in

multicultural interaction, it becomes easier to deal with it. The trick is to overcome our fears.

Carla needs to learn self-confidence. If she were more sure of herself, she wouldn't be so worried about what others thought of her. Sally had that confidence, and it didn't scare friends off. Sally was a very popular student.

Self-confidence begins with liking yourself. When you like yourself, it becomes easier to transfer that liking to others. Foreign students, as we learned from Maria and Juan, face fear in a new situation. Imagine going to a foreign country, where no one knew your language and you didn't know what to do. Whom would you rather meet? Carla, Sally, or Jaime?

Even if you can't really identify with foreign students, you can still react positively for their benefit as well as yours. You don't have to like what they wear. You don't have to become their best friend. You don't even have to like them. But what did Sally do?

Think how Maria felt seeing a friendly smile. It isn't always necessary to make the effort Jaime did. Not all of us have the ability to speak a foreign language as he did. Surely all of us can smile.

CHAPTER ◇ 2

Coping with Different Languages

Learning a second language is a unique experience. It is difficult and rewarding. Most people think that learning a second language is more difficult than learning your native language, but in fact it isn't. You learn a second, third, or fourth language the same way you learned a first language.

Many people believe that learning a second language occurs through studying in class. Taking classes helps you to learn long lists of vocabulary and to conjugate verbs, but it rarely teaches you language usage.

To become fluent in any language several factors need to exist. The most important factor is the *need to communicate*. A baby needs to interact with his or her family and therefore learns that first language. If the baby wants food, it quickly learns how to ask for it. The baby has had no vocabulary lists to memorize, no tests, no verbs to conjugate. The baby learns because he listens and watches and associates words with actions and objects. When Mom reaches for a cookie and says, "Do you want a cookie?" the baby learns that the tasty round object is a cookie.

This is an oversimplified version of how we learn language, but it will help us if we understand and remember how we learned our first language when we want to understand a second language. You will learn another language if you need to survive.

For example, in Chapter 1, North High had very few Spanish-speaking students. Maria and Juan will learn English and probably be fairly fluent in a short time. They need to know English to interact with other students, to learn in school, and probably to do business in the community as well.

In contrast, some Hispanic students come to the United States and enter schools where most of the students speak Spanish. These students will take longer to learn English because there is no critical *need* for survival. They find Spanish-speaking students for friends, probably Spanish-speaking teachers, and the community conducts business bilingually, in both Spanish and English.

The fact that these students learn English more slowly concerns many Americans. The concern is based on fear. They think that if these students never learn English, the United States may have to adopt a second official language, as Canada, Switzerland, and many other countries have done.

Some Americans think these students don't learn English because they are stupid. They say such things as, "My grandfather came to the U.S. and didn't speak English—he learned it the hard way." The fact is that *anyone* who learns a second language learns "the hard way." The grandfather may have been in a school like North High. He *had* to learn English. Students in a Spanish-speaking school and community do not need to learn English to survive, and consequently learning it becomes difficult.

If these students wish to merge into mainstream American society, they do learn English. Why? Because they *need* to in order to communicate.

Need is the most critical element in learning a language. This lack of necessity to learn a foreign language is why most Americans students are not fluent in another language in spite of taking French or German or whatever in high school. Unless there is a community of French- or German-speaking people nearby that the student *needs* to interact with, it is highly unlikely that he or she will become fluent.

It is no accident that the most effective way to learn another language is to go to school in the country where that language is spoken. In the foreign country you will *need* to speak the language. In the United States you do not *need* to because English is the dominant language and spoken *everywhere*.

Americans who speak more than one language, or, as we say, are bilingual or multilingual, know the language because there is a need. Navajos on the reservation speak the Dineh language to communicate with family and friends. They speak English to communicate at school and at work and in the community. They speak both because they *need* both.

This applies to numerous ethnic groups in our country such as other Native American tribes, religious sects, and isolated communities of immigrants.

Americans who live in border communities and in city neighborhoods of new immigrants often know more than one language. They learn them because they *need* them and *use* them.

It is interesting to note that in a bilingual community not everyone is bilingual. Take Phoenix, Arizona, for example.

It has a large Hispanic community, and most of the Hispanic people are bilingual: They speak both English and Spanish. In the same community, the other ethnic groups such as the blacks, Anglos, and Native Americans do *not* speak Spanish. The reason again is *need*. English is the predominant language, so the general community does not *need* to learn Spanish.

Some, however, do learn Spanish. If they are the only Anglos on the block or if they work in a predominantly Spanish-speaking area, they *need* to learn the second language. There is that key word again: *need*.

In spite of a *need* to learn a language, it is still a difficult process. It takes time. Remember that when you were a baby it was years before you could communicate. Knowing one language helps you to learn the second faster, but you need patience and practice.

Let's look at some situations where language differences occur in multicultural interaction.

Omar sat in class and tried to concentrate on what the teacher was saying. Her English was very strange-sounding and harsh, not at all soothing like his native language.

For a brief moment, he let himself remember the sounds of home. He could almost hear the buzz of noise at the *souk*, where men selling everything from baskets to rugs to fine gold jewelry were calling out their wares.

At sunset all sound would stop except for the call to worship sung out across the city from the parapets of the Muslim towers. Omar missed that time the most.

The teacher paused and asked a student a question. Omar tried to understand the girl's answer. It was still hard for him to get used to having girls in the class. What a strange country the United States was.

He shifted in his seat trying to find a comfortable position in the tight-fitting Western clothes. He'd give anything to be able to wear the free-flowing robes of his country.

The thought made him smile. He had worn his *goutra* one day in the neighborhood. The headpiece had generated some strange reactions. Omar hadn't worn it outside his house since.

Another fifteen minutes passed, and Omar managed to concentrate on the teacher's words. He still didn't understand what was being said, but he knew that some day he would. His father had promised. He had also ordered Omar to study hard. They needed to succeed in this country. They would be shot if they returned to Lebanon.

Just as the thought crossed his mind, a siren sounded outside the classroom. Instantly Omar stood, ready to flee the building and run for cover. Sirens warned of bombs and gunfire at home.

Omar looked around. No one seemed to be alarmed. After all, they were in the United States now. Father had assured him that this country was not at war.

The siren screamed, the high-pitched sound making him nervous. What did it mean?

Suddenly everyone started moving toward the door. The teacher was giving orders. Fear grew and seemed to clutch at his heart.

The hall was packed. Bodies streamed out of every door as students left the classrooms. In a panic Omar asked those around him what was going on. They only stared at him blankly. One guy shoved him forward and growled orders.

The crowd pressed against him and forced him to move outside. Once there, it became clear that the building was being evacuated. Nada. His sister. She would be frantic.

Ever since she had seen her friend blown to bits, she panicked when the sirens blew.

Once outside, Omar was vaguely aware of lines forming on the parking lot and lawns. He ignored them as he frantically ran from one to the other searching for Nada.

Several teachers hollered at him, but he didn't know what they were saying. All he knew was that he had to find Nada and get them both to cover.

Omar dashed around the building and found more lines forming. He heard a scream and caught sight of a girl running past the teacher.

"Nada," he hollered.

Nada stopped, nearly colliding with the teacher who was chasing her.

Omar waved.

With a cry, Nada ran toward him. Omar raced as fast as he could to get to his frightened sister. They practically collided as she buried her face against his chest and wrapped shaking arms around him.

"What is it? Are they going to shoot us?"

"No," he assured her, but had no idea what to tell her.

The teacher who had been chasing Nada caught up to them and started waving her arms. Omar tried to understand but could only stare, unable to hide his fear and confusion.

You were probably able to figure out that the school was having a fire drill. The procedure is routine to us, but to Omar and Nada, who had just come from a war-torn country, the experience was terrifying.

Nothing is more frightening than to be in a situation filled with uncertainty and fear and be unable to communicate. Remember what we said earlier about need; Omar had a need to know English, but it does take time. He had not been in the United States long enough to learn to communicate.

For someone who has never learned a second language, there is this to consider also. Even if Omar and Nada had learned some English, it is doubtful that they would have remembered it in the state of anxiety they were in. During high levels of stress, most people revert to their native language. Translating becomes extremely difficult.

Understanding these things can help us to tolerate people who are new to our country and do not speak English. If you remember that they are probably frightened or nervous, thus making it even more difficult to communicate, you can improve your attitude toward them.

That is why it is important to remain calm when trying to communicate with someone who is just learning your language. If the person you're talking to gets excited or upset, that person is likely to forget any of your language that he or she might have learned.

It is also important to consider the other person. You have no idea what is in his or her head or background, which means you cannot make a judgment as to his or her actions.

Imagine how Omar must have looked to the majority of students standing around waiting for the release bell to ring. Here is this strange boy, running around frantic and yelling for his sister. How would any of those students know what was going on in Omar's head? Most American teens have never experienced war. It would be the last thought in their minds.

Not every student who comes to the United States and doesn't speak English will experience fear as extreme as that of Omar. But most will be frightened and at least frustrated. It will help those students tremendously if we have empathy for their situation and try to be helpful, not judgmental or critical.

One of the most annoying things to face is someone who is communicating in another language and is leaving you out. Let's see what happens to Lewanda and Kasandra on a biology class field trip.

The bus bounced along the dirt road. The desert animal park wasn't too much farther. Thank goodness, Lewanda thought, as she jounced around in the back of the bus.

Li and Sue Lin were yakking away. Their Oriental chatter was driving her nuts. Why had Mr. Boynton put the two Vietnamese girls together? Didn't he know they would spend the whole day speaking their crazy lingo?

It was bad enough that Li and Sue Lin were paired off, but forcing her to be in their group annoyed Lewanda. If they didn't know English, maybe she would be more understanding, but Li and Sue Lin both spoke very good English.

Sue Lin giggled.

Lewanda looked over and caught Li staring. As soon as her dark-eyed glance made contact, Li went into gales of laughter.

Lewanda clenched her fist. They were talking about her and laughing. She wanted to punch them in the face. Just because she was tall and black, they were always laughing.

With a wistful sigh, Lewanda glanced over at Kasandra. Her best friend was in a group with Elena and Leticia. Those girls spoke Spanish. Lewanda wondered if they were talking about Kasandra as Li and Sue Lin were about her.

Kasandra leaned back, and Lewanda saw her face. She was laughing. Lewanda smiled, wishing she knew what they were laughing about. They were having more fun than she was.

Behind her, Li and Sue Lin giggled again. Lewanda swung around to see their long straight hair hiding their bent heads. Disgusted, she stood up and staggered down the aisle of the bouncing bus to where Kasandra was sitting.

"Hi," she said and hoped they would squeeze together and offer her a seat.

Kasandra looked glad to see her. "What's up? Sit down, girl, before you fall on your fanny."

Elena laughed and scooted over, making room for Lewanda. "*Sientete*," she said as she patted the seat.

"*Sientete*," Kasandra repeated the Spanish, but it didn't sound much like the way Elena had said it.

Elena and Leticia started to giggle. Lewanda wanted to say something to defend her friend, but Kasandra spoke up. "What does that mean?"

"Sit down," Leticia interpreted, "and you say it like this."

She repeated the command, and so did Kasandra, who sounded better this time.

"You try it." Elena turned to Lewanda.

"No way." She laughed. "I'm not good in Spanish."

"You can learn," Leticia said. "We've been teaching Kasandra."

So that was what had been going on. Lewanda glanced over at Li and Sue Lin. It was too bad they hadn't tried to teach her some Vietnamese. Not that she wanted to learn the sing-song language. She knew Kasandra didn't care about Spanish either, but she was having fun with Elena and Leticia. They had made it a game.

* * *

It does not matter what language is being spoken. If someone is in contact with you who doesn't understand the language, it is very rude to speak in that language and shut him or her out.

Language is a form of communication. By intentionally speaking a language in front of someone who doesn't understand it, you are shutting off the means to communicate. It is the same as hanging up the phone on someone in the middle of a conversation.

Humans are very insecure, and that insecurity breeds most of the problems they face in multicultural interaction. Lewanda couldn't understand Li and Sue Lin, so her first conclusion was that they were talking about her. In fact, she was convinced that the Vietnamese girls were laughing at her.

The truth of the matter was that Li and Sue Lin were discussing something their older brother had done at a party; they were embarrassed to tell Lewanda, so they had used their native language.

Obviously, it was not an appropriate time to discuss the problem. Knowing a language that no one around you knows is convenient at times because you can tell secrets. But telling secrets in front of others has never been a polite practice. Because of our insecurities, we always jump to the conclusion that the secret is about us.

Elena and Leticia shared their language. Kasandra may not become fluent in Spanish because she doesn't need the language, but what are her feelings about Spanish now? She probably has a positive attitude, and when she hears Spanish she'll have pleasant memories.

Lewanda will have bad memories of Vietnamese and will be less tolerant of those who speak it. Li and Sue Lin missed out on an opportunity to be good ambassadors of their culture.

It is important to remember how Lewanda and Kasandra felt as we deal with someone who doesn't know our language. It isn't always necessary to translate every word. That becomes tedious. But efforts should be made to include everyone so that they will not develop negative feelings.

There are many ways to communicate: sign language, pictures, pantomime. Can you think of others?

Learning a second language is a very rewarding experience and can broaden your view of the world. Each culture communicates its thought patterns and world view through its language. Let's look at Bobby Redhouse and see how he views the world with the language of his Navajo culture.

Bobby Redhouse stepped outside his hogan. The desert sun beat down on his back, warm and soothing to his tense nerves. He couldn't find his notebook. It had all his project research in it, and the project was due on Monday. He needed to find it soon.

For several minutes he stood and thought about all the places he had been that day. He knew he had had the notebook at school, and he was positive he had carried it off the bus. So it had to be somewhere around here or maybe at Tommy Yazzie's place. He had gone by there to help with the roundup.

Bobby Redhouse shook his head. No. It couldn't be at Tommy's. He had just come from there, and he and his friend had searched the area carefully.

"If you can't find it," Tommy had said, "why don't you go to your grandfather. He will tell you where it is."

Bobby Redhouse glanced toward the red cliff that jutted into the blue Arizona sky. His grandfather lived at its base.

The *hataali* or medicine man would know how to find the notebook, but Bobby Redhouse wanted to be sure he had tried everything himself before asking for advice.

Again he searched the hogan, the house, and the barns. He asked his mother and sisters, but they hadn't seen it. At dusk he told his family that he would visit the *hataali*.

His mother wrapped up some fry bread, and Bobby Redhouse found a suitable gift for his grandfather. As he headed toward the cliff, a sense of excitement began to build. His grandfather lived and practiced the ways of The People, the old ways. Bobby Redhouse always learned something interesting when he spent time with his grandfather.

The hike didn't take long. The sun was about to set when he approached his grandfather's hogan.

"*Yaá tá ééh*," he greeted him.

His grandfather welcomed him into the hogan. His hair was tied in a traditional knot, and a silver belt with a large turquoise stood out among the folds of his red shirt. A peace settled over Bobby Redhouse.

Slipping into the ancient language of the Navajo, Bobby Redhouse explained his problem. When his grandfather nodded, Bobby Redhouse knew that Grandfather would find his notebook if he did everything exactly as he was told.

It didn't take long to gather the bags that held the special corn pollen. Carefully, Grandfather fashioned a design on the earthen floor, using the pollen like a dry-sand painting. As it sifted through his gnarled fingers, he began to chant the old *hatals* or *sings* of The People.

Bobby Redhouse stared at the design as his mind focused on the words of the chant. He had heard them many times before, and the ancient sounds soothed him. Finally the design was complete. Grandfather stopped chanting and ordered Bobby Redhouse to cover the windows and make the room very dark.

Not a sound could be heard. It was so quiet that Bobby Redhouse could hear his own heart beat with a steady thump. His breath came in rushes as he sat very still.

He couldn't see it, but he knew the design was in front of him. He tried to picture it in his mind, and then he tried to picture the notebook. Once he thought he saw it, but he couldn't make out enough of what was in the background to figure out where it was.

Patiently Bobby Redhouse waited. He knew better than to make a sound. Grandfather would need perfect quiet.

Suddenly Grandfather moved. Bobby Redhouse strained not to jump up until his grandfather called.

It seemed to take forever. Bobby Redhouse stared at the spot where the design was, knowing better than to look at the *hataali*. Doing so would be disrespectful.

"Come, my son. We will go out and gaze at the stars," Grandfather spoke, his voice low and quiet.

Bobby Redhouse, like his people, did not like being outside at night where evil lurked, but he felt safe with Grandfather. He stood and stretched stiff limbs before following the *hataali* outside.

The stars glittered in the black sky. Grandfather stood in the yard, his head tilted back as he gazed at the spectacular view. Bobby Redhouse stared too.

His grandfather spoke, his voice cutting into the silence. "You were in a tractor today."

Bobby Redhouse's head jerked up as he stared. How did he know? Then he thought back and remembered. He had set his notebook on the back bumper while he tinkered with the engine. He wanted to tear back home and get it, but that would be rude and disrespectful.

Instead he spoke to his Grandfather. "My notebook is on the tractor. It is there."

Grandfather nodded and turned, beckoning Bobby Redhouse to follow him back inside the hogan.

Together they gathered the pollen and tossed some to the six directions. When they had finished, Grandfather opened his packages and he and Bobby Redhouse ate.

In the Navajo culture, mental telepathy is often used to locate lost items. It is an ancient art tied to the language and culture of Bobby Redhouse's family.

What would you have done if you had lost the notebook? How many of you would have sought the kind of help Bobby Redhouse did?

If the *sings* were not a part of your language and culture, you wouldn't even think to use that method. Do you see how knowing more than one language can help you? It gives you more ways to look at a problem. It gives you an added perspective on life.

Before you make fun of people who speak another language, consider that they probably know more than you do.

Each culture and language has a set of customs and a base of knowledge. Many things are the same in any language, but many ways, as we have seen here, are very different.

People who become bilingual have definite advantages. They won't be caught in a frightening situation like Omar and Nada. They won't feel left out like Lewanda. They will have more than one way to deal with life.

Because of this, let us consider what other people who speak different languages must be feeling as we interact with them. They may be frightened, confused, or feeling ostracized. But also consider that they may have no idea what you are trying to communicate if their language and culture are completely foreign to yours.

Consider how you would react in those situations, and you will understand why you need patience in dealing with others.

CHAPTER ◇ 3

Coping with Different Faiths

The Constitution of the United States provides for religious freedom. In fact, the first immigrants to America from Europe were seeking a place where they could worship as they wished. Because so many came for that purpose and because the Colonies were settled by many religious sects, the right to religious freedom evolved.

Americans have always guarded that right. Allowing people to worship as they wish requires that Americans tolerate religious differences. That is very difficult to do. However, interaction occurs, and the need to function as a country requires that we all get along. Consequently, most Americans have learned to accept the fact that people worship in many ways and have the right to do so.

In isolated incidents, interaction causes problems. Sometimes neighborhoods are segregated by religion. This physical division can create problems because it becomes easy to distinguish a religious sect and therefore discriminate against it.

Some religious groups further segregate themselves by unusual customs or dress. It is easy to distinguish Hasidic Jews by their long braids and black robes. The Amish dress in eighteenth-century style and operate their farms with eighteenth-century tools. Hare Krishnas are easily recognized by their shaved heads and orange robes.

Most religions in our country, however, have no major distinguishing characteristics. Religious practices are usually very personal, and by looking at the average American you cannot tell his or her religion. Also, because of the personal nature of religion, most people don't discuss their faith. That makes interaction a delicate and sensitive matter.

In school and at work, you will interact with people of different faiths. Unless they observe noticeable customs or dress, you probably won't know their faith. If you are just casually interacting, such as merely being in the same class with someone, knowing his or her faith doesn't really matter.

It's when relationships become more intimate that religious differences begin to affect interaction. Let's look at three friends who are planning a party.

"This baseball game is going to be the best of the season," Sharon declared as she shrugged back her long blonde hair. "So we'd better plan this party to be super."

Judith stared at Sharon and, instead of thinking about the party, wished she had straight hair like that. Her dark mop of curls framed her pixie-like features, but she wasn't aware how charming the combination was. She was too busy wishing she had something different.

Martha, who sat on the twin bed opposite both girls, wasn't thinking about hair at all. She wanted to get the party planned so she could go home and get her homework done. Bob was coming over tonight to take her to Mass for Ash Wednesday. If she wanted to go with him instead of her family, she had to finish all her assignments.

"What shall we have to drink?" Martha tried to get the planning committee back on track. "Everyone's going to be thirsty after all that shouting."

"Especially when we do our new routine," Sharon giggled. "We're going to knock them off the benches with our flips."

"You're flipped," Judith teased. "Everyone's going to be so busy watching Bob, they won't notice us cheerleaders."

Martha looked at Judith and smiled. She was crazy about Bob, but going steady with the all-star pitcher in the State did have its drawbacks. He was always attracting more attention than she cared for. Even though as a cheerleader she had to get up in front of the fans, she was basically a quiet person. She preferred dates alone with Bob, but because of his popularity those were few and far between. Tonight would be one of them, so she was anxious to hurry along with this meeting.

"Can we get sodas from your Dad's store, Sharon, or should we make punch?" Martha asked.

Sharon stopped staring at the posters in Judith's bedroom and turned to her friends. "Dad'll give us the sodas at wholesale price."

"Let's do that," Judith advised. "They'll be easier to serve, and figuring the hours we'd spend mixing punch and buying paper cups, we'll come out ahead."

"The guys won't be able to spike it either," Martha commented, thinking that would be a good thing. She didn't want to worry about Bob drinking, especially with

Lent beginning. He had promised to give up alcohol for the period of fasting. Maybe if he got out of the habit for the forty days he wouldn't start up again after Easter.

"I like spiked punch," Judith was saying. "But I suppose we'd better play it straight since this is a school-sponsored party."

"My parents would have a fit if I couldn't be a cheerleader." Sharon began playing with one of Judith's lace pillows. "Remember what happened during football season? Mr. Phillips is going to be watching us real close."

Martha groaned. A discussion about the high school principal could go on for hours. Quickly she brought the subject back to the party. "What about the food? Let's have chips and dips. I can make popcorn."

"Yum." Sharon learned back on the bed and tossed the pillow in the air. "Let's have pizza—the combination special with everything on it, sausage, pepperoni, anchovies."

Martha looked at Judith and started to protest, then changed her mind. If she told Sharon she didn't want pizza with meat on it, she'd have to explain why. No way would she leave Bob and herself open to ridicule. Last year when Bob had taken her on a double date with one of his friends from the team they had had a horrible experience.

Sharon's voice faded as Martha remembered that awful date. They had gone to Pizza Hut after a movie. It was a Friday in Lent. Bob's friend had wanted to split a large pizza, but when Bob and Martha had insisted on no meat, Bob's friend had become angry and made a big scene in the crowded restaurant. At least Bob didn't hang around with him anymore.

The incident had taught her a lesson. Because she liked Sharon and Judith, she wouldn't say a word. If they wanted pizza, she and Bob could pick off the meat before they ate it. No big deal.

Judith's voice cut into her thoughts. "What do you think, Martha?"

Martha blinked and tried not to let them know she hadn't been paying attention. "It doesn't matter to me," she lied as she shrugged.

"Well, it matters to us," Judith stated.

Martha was surprised by the determination in Judith's tone. "It's against my religion to eat pork. There will be others at the party who are Jewish. I think you ought to take that into consideration."

Martha straightened on the edge of the bed, instantly alert. She glanced around the room that looked so much like her own. Twin beds took up most of the room, and they were covered by lacy pink bedspreads. The pattern was similar to Martha's, only her bedspreads were yellow. Posters lined the walls, and makeup covered the dressing table. Photos were tucked into edges of the mirror.

Everything looked so much the same, but Judith was saying she was Jewish. Martha stared at the cheerleader she thought she knew so well.

"I'm Presbyterian," Sharon stated, "and we don't have all those rules. What about you, Martha?"

Pink flushed Martha's cheeks as she tried to decide how to answer. She wasn't sure she had Judith's courage. Yet, since Judith had spoken up, what could Sharon say?

"I agree with Judith," Martha finally took a deep breath and spoke. "We should take into consideration who will be at the party. Bob and I are fasting for Lent, and we can't eat meat on Friday."

"Are you Catholic?" Sharon's eyes grew wide.

Martha nodded.

"I thought they changed that rule about meat on Friday," Judith said in a questioning tone.

Because Judith's expression was serious and not critical,

Martha explained. "During Lent we follow the old way."

"That *is* a problem," Sharon admitted. "Shall we skip the pizza?"

"We don't have to," Judith said. "Let's just order different kinds. There may be vegetarians, for all we know. We can order vegetarian pizzas, all-beef pizzas, and the combos for you decadent Protestants."

Her last comment was teasing, and when Sharon threw the pillow at her friend all three girls laughed.

Judith and Sharon eased a touchy situation with humor. Imagine how the scene would have ended if any of the girls had taken offense. It could have become an unpleasant situation like the one Bob and Martha had faced on their double date.

When planning a party, or even just inviting friends over, if you don't know their religious affiliation it is always wise to consider all possibilities. In our country it is usually impossible to know a person's religion unless it is discussed.

The girls came up with a plan to provide something for everyone. In that way each person could make a choice of food without attracting unwanted attention.

No one likes to be singled out or embarrassed by being publicly obliged to refuse to eat something or do something because of their beliefs. When your beliefs are not considered, it is important to assert yourself and explain. Martha was afraid to tell her friends about her dietary restrictions. By speaking up, Judith was able to save herself and her Jewish friends the embarrassment and unpleasant situation of not being able to eat the food.

Food restrictions are only one of the differences one can encounter while interacting with members of other religions. Behavior and customs are also affected. For example, Seventh Day Adventists worship on Saturday, as do Jews and some Christian denominations. Some religions prohibit dancing or wearing certain clothing. Others have restrictions on activities.

When you are interacting with strangers it is always wise to keep an open mind to these differences. It will prevent misunderstandings and hurt feelings.

Some religions have strict codes of behavior as well as values and ethics. The following is an example of the Amish practice of nonviolence. Let's see what happens when Seth and Lizbeth encounter outsiders of their faith or, as they call them, "the English."

The rhythmic motion of the carriage as it jolted down the lane lulled Seth into a sense of peace. He liked the clip-clop beat of the horses' hooves on the hard-packed dirt road. The summer heat had hardened the surface so that it was almost as smooth as the paved roads of "the English."

Ahead a fox scurried across the road and quickly slid into the tall grass. Seth glanced at Lizbeth to see if she'd seen the furry animal. His sister smiled, and Seth chuckled. "See, Little Fox. There goes your namesake, hurrying to mischief."

Lizbeth frowned, but it didn't have the right effect, not the way her blue eyes twinkled with amusement.

"You're just like her," Seth teased. "Always thinking up clever tricks to play on the little ones."

"They like the games, Seth Yoder, and so do you," Lizbeth reminded him.

Seth agreed, but he didn't say so. It wouldn't do to let his sister know he appreciated her humorous behavior. She would start in on him, and then what would he do? He much preferred that her antics be directed at the younger children. He decided to change the subject.

"When we get to town, I'll drop you off at the grocer's. You can shop there while I go to the hardware store and pick up the things for Father."

Lizbeth readily agreed, and Seth chuckled. He knew she'd spend half of her time looking at the bolts of cloth sold to "the English." They weren't allowed to wear the splashy prints and vivid stripes, but he knew Lizbeth couldn't resist looking at the array of bright colors.

"They are like the flowers in Grandpa's meadow," she had told Seth when he'd found her fingering the soft fabrics.

He didn't mind. Lizbeth never questioned her faith or the rules of their community. She simply appreciated the color much the way she did a meadow in spring. The elders wouldn't understand, so Seth never mentioned it.

It didn't take long to shop at the hardware store. Mr. Jones had been supplying the farmers for years and knew exactly what they needed. He joked and teased in his usual boisterous manner, which made Seth feel comfortable even though the man was "English."

Seth drove back to the grocery and began tying the horses to the hitching post. Cars whizzed past with their noisy engines and smelly exhaust, but Seth ignored them. He was picturing the new shed he and his father were going to build.

Out of his side vision, he saw Lizbeth wave from the doorway and knew she had finished also. Good. He was anxious to return and get started on his project.

"Well, well. Look what we have here."

The masculine voice sent warning signals zinging through Seth's head. He'd heard that voice before. He swung around and saw Alan Norton and Larry Holmes, standing one on each side of Lizbeth. His muscles tensed as he quickly climbed the stairs and stood beside his sister.

"Come on, Lizbeth. Let's get the supplies."

Lizbeth led the way indoors and showed Seth the box filled with her purchases. Seth saw her lips move and knew she was silently praying. He thought of a few of his own. Alan Norton had a mean streak a mile long. His favorite pastime was harassing Seth and his friends.

"You go out and get in the wagon," Seth advised. "Keep hold of the reins in case the horses get restless."

They both knew what would make them bolt. Alan had jabbed them in the hind quarters during their last visit. Before that, he'd thrown stones.

Seth watched Lizbeth as she passed the two boys and hurried to the wagon. He followed close behind and prayed that the boys would let him go peaceably.

They didn't. Just as Seth came even, Alan stuck out his booted foot, hoping to send Seth flying. Seth was prepared and quickly sidestepped. A compelling urge to turn around and deck the two boys swelled within him, but he managed to suppress it. From all the manual labor on the farm, he was strong. He would probably hurt them, maybe even kill one. Seth shuddered at the thought and hurried to put the box in the back of the wagon.

Alan began shouting insults, but those were easy for Seth to ignore. He had heard them all his life. As he climbed into the wagon and guided the horses out of town, he thanked God that the incident had remained minor.

"Why do they keep threatening us?" Lizbeth asked the eternal question. "We don't do anything to them."

Seth sighed as he slapped the reins on the rumps of the horses. "It makes them feel superior, I guess."

"How does harassing us make them superior?" Lizbeth demanded. "I think it makes them pitiful."

"Who can explain the ways of 'the English'," Seth muttered as they silently rode home.

Seth's code of ethics, based on his religion, required that he not react to violent behavior thrown at him. How would you have reacted to Alan Norton? Do you see how religious values dictate our behavior? What we believe is what we are.

Sometimes it is difficult to understand other religions. They may be so different from ours that we can't comprehend why people act the way they do.

Often, lack of understanding causes intolerance. Alan would not respect Seth's ethic of nonviolence and continually tried to goad him into breaking it. There are many psychological reasons for prejudice, and they often include a poor self-image. Insecurity, anger, and self-hatred often motivate people to act cruelly toward others.

How do you think Alan Norton feels inside? What does he have to gain by intolerance? Is that attitude necessary? Perhaps Alan feels insecure and thinks his actions will impress his peers. Perhaps he is from a family that practices child abuse, and Alan feels anger toward people who appear contented.

The roots of prejudice go deep, and the way to overcome them is to try to understand. It is not always easy to understand other faiths.

Mainstream America is from predominantly Western civilizations such as the European countries that evolved from the Greco-Roman Empire. It is usually easy to relate to peers of the Protestant, Catholic, and Jewish faiths. The problems of understanding often come when we confront totally different faiths that derive from foreign cultures: Hinduism, Buddhism, Islam, and other Eastern cultures have religious practices very different from most of ours.

In the confusion of such variety, religious groupings change. Sometimes they blend two or more faiths that are in contact with each other. For example, the Native American Church in the Southwest is a blend of Christianity with the way of the Navajo.

When you come in contact with different faiths, it may lead to confusion or doubts about your own. You need not be afraid of that. It never hurts a person to be exposed to the variety of cultures and faiths that make up our country.

Problems arise when you cannot accept that other people have different faiths and you do not allow them the freedom to practice. Problems also arise if you are not secure in your own beliefs; the doubts can cause you unrest or confusion.

The best thing to do when that happens is to discuss the matter with your parents or religious counselors.

The most important thing to remember is that under our Constitution all faiths have a right to exist in this country. The fact that our population is a blend of peoples from many countries and cultures makes it inevitable that different faiths will emerge.

You have the right to choose how you want to believe. You have the obligation to respect the beliefs of others. That does not mean you have to agree with their beliefs. It merely means that you allow them to practice them in peace.

CHAPTER ◇ 4

Coping Across Economic Classes

In the United States, we do not have a rigid and defined class structure. Different economic classes exist. We have poverty, the middle class, and the wealthy class. The difference between our economic system and those of other countries is that we can move from one category to another.

If you are born to a poor family, you are not required to remain in that state your whole life. If you choose, you can move up the economic ladder and virtually go as high as your drive will take you. Classic stories are heard every day: Some man or woman comes from a poor, uneducated family and overcomes all obstacles to make it to the top.

This class mobility is what attracts many people to our country. In many societies you cannot move from one class to another. If you're born in a low class, you remain there your entire life.

Moving from one class to another involves many changes.

It is not just a matter of money. Cultural differences exist between the classes, and if you wish to move into another class, you need to learn them.

Examples abound of people amassing large amounts of money but never being accepted into the upper class. Lottery winners are an example. Suddenly they have a fortune, but if they do not acquire the culturally accepted behavior, they are rarely accepted by the upper class.

An example of this can be seen in a person's home. A lottery-winning family from the economically lower class moves to a new house in an upper-class neighborhood. They've always kept old cars around for spare parts to keep the family car running. If they continue this practice in the new neighborhood, they will not be accepted. They may have the money to rank them in the class of the wealthy, but they don't act the part.

Drug dealers are another prime example. They may have tremendous wealth, flashy clothes, and expensive cars but their criminal life-style prevents them from entering the status of the elite.

Education is also part of the class system in America. It is in fact the means by which most Americans move upward in status. Despite exceptions, the more education you have, the higher you are able to go.

Sometimes a high degree of education alone will give you upper-class status. A space scientist or a Nobel Prize-winning physicist may not have much wealth, but accomplishments put him or her in the realm of the elite.

The factors that determine your class can all be acquired. A famous movie producer was the son of immigrants; instead of going to school, he worked as a child because they were so poor. He loved movies, and in his teens he left home and hitchhiked to Hollywood. At the gates of a studio, he promised himself that he would someday make movies. As he says, "By age twenty-five, I produced my first movie."

This man believed in himself. He did not let his background stop him. He is now not only a successful movie producer, but an author and a public speaker who enjoys wealth and fame.

Everyone can become whatever they desire in this country. But as the movie producer points out, it takes hard work and determination. Financial success will not be handed to you. If it is, such as a winning lottery ticket or receiving an unexpected inheritance, you will need to change and live up to the new role in order to keep it.

The important thing to remember is that all things are possible. In the United States we are not bound by economic class. We can move up the economic ladder or move down it. The direction you take is up to you.

As teens, however, you are defined by your parents' status. It may seem that you are unable to make changes until you can get out on your own to earn more money. That is not true. There is much you can be doing toward your dreams.

Remember that money is not the only criterion. You can move up through education. Study hard so that you can go to college. Graduation often leads to higher-status jobs. Remember also that behavior and cultural values play roles. Study people and learn from their behavior.

Let's look at Sean and Travis. Their parents are in the Navy in San Diego. They attend school with teens from Point Loma, a wealthy, upper-class neighborhood. Can you see how conflicts will arise from the economic differences of their families?

The bell rang, and students rushed out of the classrooms and headed toward the concessions for the midday break.

Sean shouldered his way through the crowd, looking for Travis. They had been buddies for a long time, and Sean enjoyed the kidding around when they got together. Others did too. Sean and Travis always attracted a crowd that enjoyed their jokes and laughter.

"Here he comes," someone shouted.

"Hey, man."

Sean turned toward that voice. It was Trav.

"What's up?" He slapped his friend's hand as he joined him. Already a group had formed around the tall, good-looking blond.

Sean spotted Scott in the crowd and grinned. He liked the redhead and always enjoyed his company. Scott lived in Point Loma, as did most of the students hanging around. The thing about Scott was that it didn't make much difference. He didn't act superior because his folks had big bucks. He was just one of the guys.

"Trav was telling us what happened yesterday." Scott brought Sean into the conversation. "I can just see Crystal's face."

Everyone laughed, and so did Sean. They had played a joke on the most popular girl in the sophomore class. Crystal loved a good joke as much as anyone. She had been a great sport about it, and Sean supposed that was what made her so popular.

"You got a thing for Crystal?" Scott asked.

"No way," Sean denied, but Travis laughed, so no one believed him.

"What's going down this weekend?" Sean asked, to change the subject. "Are you going to the game?"

"You better." Scott pretended to scowl. He was the star quarterback.

"We'll be there," Sean assured him. "Cheering for the other team."

"Hey!" Scott stiffened his shoulders as if he were going to tackle Sean. Everyone laughed.

"Wanna go cruising tonight?" Trav asked. "Let's go to Pacific Beach and check out the action."

Several guys agreed right away, but Scott reminded them that he had practice. Trav turned to Sean.

"You going?"

Sean hesitated. Pacific Beach was his favorite hangout. Something was always going on—skaters, cyclists, volley ball games, kites, and surfing. Of course there were always girls.

Reluctantly he said, "I can't go. I've got an Algebra test tomorrow."

"Hey, man," Trav protested. "I'm driving."

Again temptation lured him. Travis had a mean-looking Trans Am. His father couldn't afford to buy him a car like most of their friends had, so Travis had worked his tail off all summer to earn the money himself.

"Studying is a drag," claimed one of the guys standing next to Scott. "I'm for cruising."

Sean smiled, but inside he knew he wouldn't go. "Catch me after school," he told Trav. "I'll let you know then."

The bell rang, cutting off further discussion. The group split up.

"Come on, Trav," Sean motioned. "Let's get to English—your favorite teacher."

Travis groaned, and Sean chuckled. Together they walked down the corridor. Suddenly someone bumped into Travis. Sean steadied his friend and turned to the two. Greg and Doug. Sean groaned silently as he readied himself for trouble.

"Get out of the way, you Navy swabbies," Doug snarled.

Greg chimed in. "You're scum. Go back to sea where you belong."

Travis started to attack, but Sean quickly grabbed his friend's arm.

"Get lost," Sean told the seniors. "Haven't you got anything else to do?"

Doug grinned, but it was more of a snarl. "What's the matter? Afraid of getting creamed?"

The second bell rang, and Greg put in one last remark. "Not by scum like you."

With that he swung around and headed on down the corridor. Doug followed.

Sean fought the urge to run after them and bash their heads in. One look at Travis, and he knew his friend struggled with the same inner battle.

"Come on." Sean started walking away. "Don't pay any attention to them."

Travis followed, but he muttered with each step. "It isn't fair. Just because our fathers don't make big bucks, they treat us like dirt. They don't stop and think that it's our Dads who keep this country free so their . . ."

"Drop it, Trav. It's the same old thing. It wouldn't matter to them if we had tons of money. They just need someone to hassle to make themselves feel like big stuff."

Trav looked skeptical, but he calmed down. Reaching their classroom, they went in and took their seats. Sean didn't pay attention at first. He was busy thinking that he would stay home and study for the Algebra test. He was going to earn that scholarship to college. He was going to graduate and become a big-time lawyer. Then creeps like Doug and Greg would see he was somebody.

Travis and Sean were forced to interact with students in a different economic class from theirs. Not everyone made it difficult for the two boys. In fact, they were very popular because of their humor and sharp wit. But there are always people like Doug and Greg who enjoy belittling others.

The positive side of the harassment Sean suffered is that he is determined to go on to college and move up the economic ladder. He is not waiting until he graduates from high school, but is planning and studying *now* for his future.

Travis also compensated for his economic status. He wanted to have a car like his friends, so instead of enjoying the beach all summer, he worked several jobs.

You can make your economic situation fit your needs in many ways. It takes positive action and determination. Travis and Sean could have moped around and complained about their situation. Feeling sorry for yourself accomplishes nothing except to make you more unhappy.

It is important to remember that positive and sensible steps help you to move. Sometimes we don't make sensible choices. It is tempting to let our desires rule over reason. Let's see how Shelley handles the economic differences of her friends.

The shopping mall was crowded, but Shelley didn't mind. She liked the hustle and bustle of shoppers milling around from store to store. Vivid colors were displayed in the windows to tempt the passersby. Shelley liked the clothing boutiques best, but jewelry stores often caught her eye as well.

"Look at those diamonds," Shelley pointed to a sparkling necklace.

Crystal and Cindy stopped beside her and stared.

"My Mom has a necklace like that," said Crystal. "I tried it on once. It's unreal."

Cindy pointed to another necklace that had fewer diamonds but an elegant design. "My Mom's looks more like that one."

Shelley remained silent. Her mother didn't have a diamond to her name, let alone a necklace as grand as those. She glanced at her friends and tried not to let envy take control of her emotions.

She hated being poor. Her mother was divorced, and every penny she made went to house payments and the basics. Shelley worked at McDonald's so that she could buy clothes. At least she didn't look poor. Crystal and Cindy had no idea, and Shelley was careful not to let on.

Afraid her friends might ask what kind of diamonds her mother had, Shelley changed the subject.

"Look at that outfit." She pointed to the boutique across the walk. "They have the new style skirts."

Crystal's attention was immediately captured. "Let's go try some on."

Cindy quickly agreed. "I want the turquoise."

Shelley kept up with them as they crossed the mall and entered the small shop.

It didn't take long for them to find a selection of skirts to try on. Along with the skirts, they took blouses and sweaters into the fitting room.

"This is the most," Crystal said, as she modeled an outfit. "I bet Sean would take a second look if he saw me in this."

"Sean would look twice if you had on old jeans. He's crazy about you," Cindy said as she stepped in front of the mirror beside Crystal. "I'm buying this." She admired the turquoise skirt she had on.

"Shelley, have you found anything yet?" Crystal called through the slats of the dressing room door.

Had she ever! Shelley eyed the sleek skirt and top. They

were something else. They made her slim figure look terrific. She wanted this outfit.

"No, I don't think this is me," she lied. She had added up the astonishing figures on the price tags and knew she didn't have the money for it.

Before she could take off the clothes, Crystal opened the door. "Let me see! I thought for sure that outfit would look good on you."

Shelley backed up but knew it was too late.

"What do you mean? It looks fantastic," Crystal exclaimed. "Cindy, look at this. Isn't it perfect for Shelley?"

Cindy came to the door and agreed. Shelley knew they were right, but how could she tell her friends it was too much money?

"You have to buy that, Shelley! It would be perfect for the party this weekend."

Cindy *would* have to remind her of the party. The skirt and top were perfect, and she would really be with it in this outfit. Surely Scott would notice her.

"I'm taking this skirt and those two sweaters," Crystal told them. "Are you buying the turquoise one, Cindy?"

"You bet." Cindy held up that skirt and also a white one. "I think I'll take both."

A surge of envy overcame Shelley. She wished she could just come in and buy whatever she wanted as Crystal and Cindy did. It wasn't fair.

Quickly she did some mental arithmetic. She had enough money in her purse to buy the outfit. The problem was, part of that money was supposed to be for schoolbooks. She could buy the books later. It would mean she'd get behind in her assignments, but she wanted the outfit. Besides, what else could she tell Crystal and Cindy?

"I'll buy it if you think it looks that good," she told them. She'd worry about the money later.

* * *

Shelley was shopping with friends from a different economic class. Her wealthy friends didn't have to budget their money as she did. You can see the stress that created.

Do you think Shelley was wise to buy the outfit? What alternatives did she have?

Sometimes you get into situations that are difficult to get out of without bringing unwanted attention to yourself. Shelley did not want to let Crystal and Cindy know she had financial problems, and she felt pressured by her friends to buy the outfit. If you are in a situation where economic class can become a problem, try to arm yourself with the inner strength to be honest. If Shelley had simply said, "I can't afford this right now," the girls would have ceased their persuasion.

Shelley could have warned her friends at the outset, "I'll go shopping, but I'm not buying today." If she didn't want to mention money she could give several other reasons that her friends would accept. If the girls knew ahead of time, they would probably not pressure her.

In the case of clothes, it is often wise to window-shop at the exclusive boutiques. There you can see what styles and colors are in. It isn't always the clothing that makes the outfit, but how you combine and accessorize them. The boutiques use the latest styles on their mannequins. Smart shoppers can see the "in" look and find the necessary articles at less expensive stores. They can achieve the look of class by knowing how to put outfits together. No one will know the price you paid unless you tell them.

Shelley can learn ways to compensate for her lower economic status. But what if you're the one with the advantages, and you have friends with fewer material things than you? It is important that these teens learn to interact also.

Crystal and Cindy pressured Shelley because they didn't

realize her money problems. But what if they had known? What choices did they have when interacting with Shelley? They could make matters worse or they could be understanding.

Let's meet Chad, who is from a wealthy family. He lives at Lake Tahoe, a famous ski resort. His best friend, Steve, also lives at Tahoe but is from an average working-class family. How does Chad handle the situation?

The gymnasium echoed as Coach shouted out the drill pattern for lay-ups. Chad watched Steve closely as he maneuvered into position. The ball bounced on the hardwood floor as Steve dribbled toward the basket.

"Now," Chad shouted. He quickly swiped at his shorts to dry the sweat off his fingers.

Steve passed the ball and Chad stepped in front of Mark. He had it. In a flash he was on his way with perfect control of the ball.

As he dribbled, Chad kept an eye on Steve. Mark tried to stay between Chad and Steve, but Chad was too quick for that. As soon as Steve was in position, Chad bounced the ball beside Mark's feet, which completed the pass to Steve.

They had the game now. Steve gave it his all as he went for the lay-up. His tall, lean body was poetry in motion as he slam-dunked the basketball for the winning points.

Chad jumped with a shout. Coach roared approval. The rest of the team cheered. Everyone, that is, except Mark.

Chad caught a glimpse of the senior before he stomped off to the locker room. He was mad. Chad shrugged, knowing that Mark was jealous of Steve's playing ability. Let him pout. It was only practice.

Before he could think anymore about Mark, Steve and Chad were bombarded by their teammates.

"Great slam-dunk!" Chad slapped Steve on the back.

"You set me up perfect. I couldn't have done it without that pass." Steve was always generous about sharing the glory. Chad supposed that was part of the reason he liked Steve.

Coach let them calm down before he gave a last-minute pep talk. "You boys rest up. It's going to be a tough game tomorrow night."

Everyone cheered and hollered as they ran one last lap around the gym before heading for the locker room.

It didn't take long for the room to steam up. Chad quickly showered and put on his thermals. It was not cold in there, but he knew it was snowing outside.

"Anyone know how many inches have fallen?" Mark asked as he sat on the bench pulling on his snow boots.

"It's been snowing since noon," Steve commented.

Steve was hanging up his sweats, so he didn't see the glare Mark sent his way. Chad saw it and wondered what he was up to now.

"I've got an idea," Mark hollered.

Several guys groaned, but most listened. Mark was still a leader, and there was always action around him.

"Let's all go to Heavenly Valley this weekend. Ski conditions will be perfect."

Chad thought of the soft powder and was about to agree until he spotted the slight frown on Steve's forehead.

"I'll drive," one of the team offered his van.

"No way. I'm taking my own wheels."

"That's because you hope to pick up on some action," Mark teased. Everyone knew that the female tourists idolized the local skiers.

Chad was about to agree to go when Mark started talking again.

"Hey, Steve. You coming with us this time?"

"No." Steve shook his head.

"Why not? You never come with us."

Mark's badgering annoyed Chad. Several other guys became silent and turned back to their lockers. They all knew that Steve couldn't afford the expensive downhill skis nor the lift tickets. Mark had deliberately set out to embarrass Steve.

Chad spoke up. "Count me out on Heavenly. I've got plans already." He stepped over to Steve and said confidentially but in a voice he made sure all heard, "Dad has a friend flying in for the weekend. We're taking him out in the helicopter. Do you want to cross-country with us?"

Chad knew Steve had cross-country skis. Steve's eyes lit up, as did everyone's in the locker room.

"The pilot's going to drop us off in virgin snow. We'll ski in from the top."

Chad knew that every guy in the gym would give anything to trade places with Steve right now. That was exactly what he wanted.

"Sure, I'll go." Steve grinned. "Let me know where and when."

"I'll call tonight after I talk to Dad," Chad told him.

The players went back to discussing their individual plans. Chad whistled as he left the locker room. Friends had to stick together.

How did Chad, who had all the economic advantages, react to Steve's predicament? He could have gone on to Heavenly Valley and left Steve on his own, but instead he took a potentially embarrassing situation and eased Steve through it with his generous offer.

Chad could have offered to pay for Steve's lift ticket, but would that have accomplished the same thing? Why?

If you are from a better economic situation than your friends, remember to consider their feelings. Hurt pride can sometimes cause more damage than poverty.

No matter what economic class you come from, and no matter whether you're interacting with someone in a higher or lower position, it is always necessary to consider people's feelings. It helps to understand why people act the way they do so that you don't misunderstand others and they don't misunderstand you.

The important thing to remember when interacting across economic class lines is that in the United States nothing is guaranteed or static. You can move to any point on the ladder you choose. The decision is yours to make and the responsibility is yours to act.

CHAPTER ◇ 5

Overcoming Prejudice

Prejudice by definition is an opinion formed beforehand without adequate basis. In a society as complex as ours, we are exposed to many opinions. Often we base our beliefs on information we obtain from others. The problem with this is that the foundations for those beliefs may not be sound. The result is prejudice instead of an informed opinion.

American society is prone to use statistics and polls to form opinions. There is danger in this, because statistics can be made to indicate whatever the person using them wants. Whoever writes the questions puts in his own bias and prejudice to make the figures prove his theories.

Our population is exposed to an overwhelming amount of information. Television, movies, and radio have brought world affairs into our lives. It may seem that we are informed, but there is real danger that we could be forming prejudices.

How many of us are experts on all of the issues dealt with in world news? Most of us aren't even aware of the full extent of local news. Therefore, we are forming opinions without adequate basis. That is prejudice.

Suppose you are from a small town in rural America. In this town there are no black families. Your only exposure to blacks is what you see in movies and on television. If you watch the national news and continually see young blacks arrested, shot, and involved in inner-city drug busts, what opinion of blacks are you forming?

It is true that there are gangs and that blacks are among the many people involved. But what you don't see and what is not reported on television news are all the black families that lead healthy, wholesome lives. The news reports only the unusual.

True, a few television shows and a few movies portray blacks in a positive light. These, however, are fiction. The news is real life. Which presentation is the more believable?

You don't have to live in rural America for this prejudice to form. Americans who live in integrated cities struggle with the same prejudices because of their limited exposure to who blacks are.

This is just one example of how the media can influence your thinking. It wasn't long ago that Americans had a distorted view of Native Americans because of their roles in Western movies. Think of other cultures presented in the news and assess your opinion of them.

How do you view East Indians? Is all of India poverty-stricken and crowded? What is South Africa like? Is it a country of continuous riots and conflict? Are all Colombians involved in drug cartels? Are all Central Americans communists?

If you answered yes to any of those questions, you are a

victim of prejudice. You have based your opinions on a limited presentation of facts.

It is impossible to be an expert on every subject. So how do you overcome prejudice? Recognizing it is the first step. If you realize that your opinion is based on limited facts, you will be more open-minded to accept additional information.

The next step is to avoid taking action on your beliefs until you are sure of all the facts. It is one thing to sit in your living room and mistakenly believe that all blacks are involved in drugs. It is another matter for you to think you can do something about it without first checking into the situation more thoroughly.

Danny found out the hard way what could happen when he and his friends decided to act before they discovered the true facts.

Rain drizzled outside, but Danny paid little attention to the gray skies and wet weather. It was normal climate for the Pacific Northwest. Besides, it didn't matter if it was raining; he was headed for the shopping mall.

Danny dashed from his car and through the smoke-tinted doors. It was warm inside. Bright lights and colorful displays invited the shoppers in. He spotted his friends at the fountain and hurried toward them.

Kurt was lounging against the direction sign. He was wearing his camouflage fatigues and a forest-green T-shirt. His blond hair was cut short.

Pat didn't look much different except that his T-shirt was khaki and had a patch of an American flag on the back.

Danny joined them, wishing his camouflage pants had been clean. He'd worn blue jeans instead. Maybe he'd buy another pair today so he wouldn't be in this bind next weekend.

"Sorry I'm late," he apologized as he joined his friends. "Traffic into the city was a..."

"Man, don't you know it," Pat interrupted. "It took forever to find a parking place."

"Everyone's coming into the big city," Kurt agreed.

"School starts next week," Danny pointed out.

"Ugh! Don't remind me."

"I don't mind the crowds. In fact, take a look over there."

Danny glanced where Pat was pointing. He whistled between his teeth.

Kurt straightened. "She's some looker."

In unison, they began to follow the long-legged redhead until she entered a shop.

It didn't matter. There were plenty more where she came from. The mall was packed with the opposite sex. That was why Danny and his friends liked to hang out there.

For over an hour they cruised the lower level and then moved up to the second. Suddenly Kurt stopped and grabbed Pat's arm. Danny backed up and tried to find out what they were staring at.

At first he couldn't see anything unusual. Kurt whispered to Pat, and then Danny saw him. A black man. His stomach tightened as he wondered what his friends were going to do.

Kurt and Pat stood still until the man moved. Slowly they began to follow as he strolled toward the big department store at the end of the walk.

Nervous and edgy, Danny kept pace with his friends. He knew how much they hated blacks. Actually, they hated anyone who wasn't white, but they especially hated blacks. Danny didn't want any trouble.

Maybe he would disappear, he thought as he watched the tall, lean man take easy strides. Danny hadn't seen many blacks. There were none in the suburb where his family lived. Maybe if he had known some, they wouldn't look so frightening to him now.

Kurt and Pat quickened their pace. Danny lagged behind and tried to distract them.

"Hey," he called. "Look at those shirts. Let's try some on."

Kurt ignored Danny. Pat turned and motioned for him to catch up.

"Keep up," he muttered as Danny came beside him.

"What are we trailing him for?" Danny asked, but he knew. Kurt was watching for an excuse to cause trouble.

It came suddenly. A woman and her small daughter came out of a side store. The little girl wasn't watching where she was going and ran into the black man. He swung around and accidentally knocked the packages out of the woman's hand. Both bent to help the little girl, who was crying.

"Get your filthy hands off her!" Kurt ran up to the black.

Danny froze, embarrassed and afraid.

The black man slowly stood, holding his hands in front of him.

"Don't give me any trouble now." He stepped away from the woman, who was holding her daughter.

The packages were lying forgotten on the ground. Pat moved beside Kurt and faced the man, his hands balled into fists.

"What're you doing?" Kurt scowled. "We don't want your kind here, knocking down little girls—attacking women."

Kurt sounded tough. Danny stared, wondering where the mean look had come from. He had never seen Kurt look so violent.

The black man didn't move, but stood and held Kurt's gaze. He didn't seem frightened—only wary. Danny would have been shaking in his boots if Kurt and Pat had him surrounded like that.

"You boys back off," the man said. He sounded calm, but determined. "I don't want to fight with you. I don't want anyone hurt."

Kurt stepped forward; a sound close to a growl was his only response.

The black man motioned to the woman. "You better take your little girl and move away."

His voice was still—calm. Danny could feel sweat trickling down his back.

Kurt and Pat hurled several more insults, but still the black man did not move. Danny willed him to run. Didn't he realize it was three against one?

Suddenly Kurt attacked, but the man easily sidestepped the blow.

"Go home, boys," he repeated. "Before anyone gets hurt."

"You go back to the hole you came from," Kurt taunted. He held his shoulders in a threatening stance. "We don't want drugs or gangs in our town."

"You don't know what you're talking about, boy."

"Boy?" Pat joined Kurt. "Who are you to call us boy? We're bigger men than you can hope to be."

The situation was worsening. The man refused to leave, and Danny knew that Kurt and Pat would never back down. Danny wondered if he was brave enough to join his friends in a fight. They were strong: He probably wouldn't need to.

The man tried to reason with Kurt and Pat, but they were past that stage. He made sense, too. Danny wished they would listen to him.

"Just everybody back away, and I'll go on to finish my shopping."

Danny decided to speak. "He's right, Kurt. It was an accident. Let's go."

The man turned toward Danny, which was a mistake. As soon as his glance moved away, Kurt attacked. Suddenly fists were flying and bodies falling. It was over in two seconds flat. Kurt and Pat were out cold. The man wasn't even breathing hard.

Danny backed away.

"I'm not going to hurt you." The man spoke quietly. His eyes were sorrowful, his expression weary and sad. "Go call security and have them bring some help for your friends."

Danny didn't need to be told twice. He left the man, who had begun to press a handkerchief on the cut along Kurt's jaw.

Danny found help for his friends. The police arrived, and Kurt and Pat were taken in for assault and battery but were released when the man, Mr. Stewart, didn't press charges. He did insist on talking to the boys.

Kurt didn't pay much attention. Pat may have, but Danny did. Mr. Stewart was a Marine, assigned to a Special Services Unit and trained in all forms of self-defense.

Danny, Kurt, and Pat had assumed because of his color that he was a troublemaker and involved in a gang or drugs. They didn't stop to find out that he was the son of a famous doctor and was simply shopping for his pregnant wife.

Kurt's stereotyping and obvious prejudice backfired on

him. What alternatives of behavior did the boys have? If you were Danny, what would you have thought about Mr. Stewart?

It is dangerous to prejudge other human beings. You have no idea what their background is or where they are coming from.

What do you think of Mr. Stewart's reaction? Did he handle the situation wisely? Did he exhibit any prejudicial behavior?

That man would be justified in hating these three boys. He could have hurt the boys more seriously instead of simply knocking them cold to protect himself. He could have pressed charges. What did his behavior show about him?

Often a gentle and understanding attitude can defuse prejudicial behavior. Mr. Stewart's treatment of the boys changed Danny's attitude toward blacks. Danny began to realize that he was just another man like the whites he knew at home.

If Mr. Stewart had pressed charges, pulled a knife, or sought revenge, what attitudes would he have reinforced in Danny? Do you see how an act of revenge on his part could have proved the stereotype Danny held? The act of kindness changed it.

Let's examine another incident in which prejudice influenced behavior. Jeremy and Selena, two black students, and their Chicano friend Rafael are at the downtown bus terminal waiting for the city bus that will take them to their high school.

"I wish the bus would get here," Selena said as she glanced around the crowded terminal. "I'm tired of waiting."

Several groups of students were standing around. She recognized most of them and knew that they, too, were waiting for bus 10, the run that went past South High.

"It can take as long as it wants as far as I'm concerned," Jeremy said. "I'm in no hurry to get to school."

Selena swung her glance from the crowd back to Jeremy. He looked good in the new studded vest. The black leather blended well with his dark braided hair. She smiled. She was crazy about the senior, and she thought maybe he was beginning to get serious about her.

A movement behind Jeremy caught her attention. "Look who's coming."

Jeremy swung around just as Rafael arrived. "Hey, my man, what's happening?"

"*Ese*," Rafael said as he performed the ritual hand greeting with Jeremy. Then he stepped back and smiled at Selena.

"Looking good." He winked.

Selena chuckled as her chocolate-colored skin darkened with her blush. She knew Rafael teased, trying to get a rise out of Jeremy. The plan worked.

Jeremy strutted up to Rafael, his chest thrust out and a pretend mean look on his face. "Don't you go messin' with my girl now."

Rafael made a face of mock horror and backed up. At the same moment, a woman walked behind him. Selena tried to warn Rafael, but it was too late. Fortunately Rafael was quick and caught himself up before he had knocked them both down.

The woman screamed and backed up. "Don't you touch me."

Selena bristled. The woman acted as if Rafael were dirt or worse.

"*Perdóneme*," Rafael said quickly as he reached to steady the woman.

She stepped back in alarm, her balance teetering on high heels, her briefcase waving in the air.

"Leave me alone!" Panic sounded in her voice, which was getting higher and louder, close to a scream.

Rafael quickly backed away, his hands up to show he meant no harm. Selena held her breath. She could sense the alert attention the incident had created. Everyone around them had gone suddenly still.

The woman regained her balance. Assured now that Rafael meant no harm, she clutched her briefcase close and hurried toward the door. The furtive glances she cast at the other students lounging around conveyed her fear. Selena didn't know whether to be angry, to feel pity, or just to laugh. She opted for the latter.

Jeremy's expression remained closed until he heard her laughter. Then he shook his head and draped his arm across Rafael's shoulder. "Did you see that honky woman's face? Man, she thought you were going to rape her or something."

"She wished," Rafael joked.

Selena heard the faint tones of hurt in his voice. "Don't take it personal, Rafael. She was just paranoid."

"Yeah. No sweat, man." Jeremy slugged Rafael playfully in the arm.

Rafael shook off Jeremy's hand and stood watching a commuter bus arrive. Businessmen and women filed off the bus. The men wore suits and ties. The women could have stepped out of a store window display, their hair perfect, their nails long and polished.

To her surprise, Jeremy stepped forward into the path of the exiting people. "Watch this," he said, his smile not reaching his eyes.

A woman stepped around him. A man filed past. The

line shifted over to accommodate Jeremy's presence.

Another woman came toward Jeremy. She smiled at the trio of students, her expression happy and peaceful. Jeremy waited until she passed.

The next man who came by peered furtively at the group. Fear showed in his expression. Jeremy waited until the man came even and then stepped near, a low growl coming from deep in his throat. The man jumped aside. Uncertainty showed on his face. Jeremy and Rafael laughed.

Several more people passed. Some had preoccupied looks on their faces. Others wore smiles. Jeremy let them go by.

"What are you doing?" Selena moved beside him. She didn't want him getting in any trouble. They'd ban him from the bus.

"Look at 'em," Jeremy pointed to another commuter bus emptying into the terminal. "They come from their fat-cat homes in the suburbs and act like they just entered the combat zone."

"Not all of them." Selena pointed to two men who were talking and laughing as if they were in a world of their own.

"I don't mess with them either," he told her.

"Why do you bother the others?"

"'Cause, man," Rafael explained. "It's like they expect to be robbed or mugged."

"Maybe we'll make their wish come true," Jeremy chuckled, but it was a mean-sounding laugh.

"They're such high and mighty snobs. Too good to associate with common masses."

Selena didn't like the tone of the conversation. It was getting ugly. "There's nothing to worry about here. There's only just us kids hanging around waiting for our bus."

Jeremy paid no attention. He started for another bus that was unloading passengers. "I hate their attitude," he muttered. "Makes me want to stick my fist in their face."

Bus 10 finally pulled up. Selena sighed with relief when she saw the other students getting onto the bus.

"Come on, guys. Our bus is here."

To her relief Jeremy and Rafael turned from the crowd and walked with her.

How many incidents of prejudice did you recognize in that scene? Describe the prejudice exhibited by the white business persons. Many of those people would probably be shocked if you told them they were practicing prejudicial behavior. Many people don't realize how their actions give them away.

None of the people getting off the bus said anything insulting to the students. No one did anything offensive. But it was obvious who did not trust a group of black and Chicano kids hanging around a bus terminal. The looks of fear, the tightening hold on purses and briefcases, the quick steps past the students. What does that say?

Not everyone exhibited those faulty judgments. Did Jeremy and Rafael bother everyone who passed them by? Why not?

That shows how prejudice can hurt you. If you could become like those business persons, which ones would you want to be like? The ones who are confident, smiling, and respected, or those who are fearful, anxious, and harassed?

The people from the suburbs were not the only ones exhibiting prejudicial behavior. How did Rafael and Jeremy show their prejudices?

The standard stereotype of prejudice is whites practicing it against other races. Was that the case here?

No one group or person has cornered the market on prejudice. Remember its definition. It is an uninformed opinion based on unsubstantiated facts. Jeremy and Rafael obviously had little interest in or compassion for the reasons behind the whites' behavior. They didn't stop to consider that their style of clothing was radical, their hair style wild.

Most of the prejudice in our country results from racial differences. We are also prejudiced concerning class differences, but since class is not well defined, it's easier to see differences in skin color.

Racial prejudice is the most serious, but it is not the only problem. As we saw in the last chapter, prejudice exists among religious sects. Sometimes ethnic background creates the difference. In Chicago, for example, the city is unofficially subdivided into ethnic neighborhoods: the Polish, the Irish, the Lithuanian. Those are not racial differences, but cultural.

Since prejudice occurs because of a lack of understanding, the best way to combat it is to become informed. If you need to interact with people in your community who are culturally different, you will save save yourself a lot of grief if you make an effort to learn about them and keep your mind open for understanding.

Danny learned the hard way that you can't judge people based on limited information. Selena could see the harm caused by prejudicial behavior.

Think about those situations. What alternatives were there? What behavior provoked the problems? What behavior eased the problems?

In the situations of multicultural interaction you've faced recently, what were all the ways they could have been handled? Overall, a peaceful and gentle attitude can defuse trouble and open the gates to understanding.

CHAPTER ◇ 6

Envy and Fear Destroy

We now know what prejudice is and how it works in multicultural interaction. If steps are not taken to understand those you encounter who are racially, religiously, or culturally different, serious problems can occur.

Often it is encounters involving misunderstandings, negative reactions, and violence that lead to envy and hatred.

In the last chapter Mr. Stewart forgave Danny and his friends. Consequently, Danny's opinion of blacks elevated from his former prejudiced view. What if the black man had sought revenge? It would have reinforced Danny's prejudice, and he would have learned to hate.

The prejudice at the bus terminal was more subtle but just as damaging. If those high school students continually confront people like the frightened woman and suspicious man, they will soon develop a poor self-image or do what

Jeremy and Rafael did—develop violent behavior and hatred.

When prejudice is reinforced, hatred will surely exist. Unfortunately, many incidents of misunderstanding among culturally different people establish hate. Remember the incident with Lewanda? If she had been continually shut out of conversations because they were in other languages, she would soon develop hatred toward all speakers of that language.

In the incident with Seth Yoder, Alan Norton did not understand the Amish culture and harassed Seth. Perhaps it was based on envy of Seth's peace and sense of conviction. In any event, his envy and misunderstanding fed his hatred.

Unfortunately, most of us lack Seth's firm belief in peaceful living. It takes the strength of faith to refrain from violence. In adverse situations we often act before thinking. Situations that we don't understand appear threatening, and our instinct is to react with hostility.

Often we don't seem to have much choice in our development of hatred or envy. The misunderstandings pass from generation to generation, and we have them because they are learned from our parents.

Some religious cults actually teach hatred and encourage violent behavior toward nonmembers. Unfortunately several hate cults exist in the United States. Because of our freedom and civil rights, they are allowed to exist.

To understand the dangers of hatred and envy, it is necessary to realize what exactly hatred and envy are. Let's meet two Mexican Americans, Margarita and Teresa, and see how they treat a white classmate in a soccer game during high school P.E.

* * *

Teresa raced down the soccer field and ducked past Barbara. She was in the clear to kick in a goal. Quickly she turned and signaled her friend and teammate, Margarita, who got the message. Margarita kicked the ball, but it never arrived.

From behind her, Barbara raced in front of Teresa and stole the ball. Before Teresa could react, Barbara was dribbling down to the opposite end of the field.

Barbara's teammates reacted promptly, and another goal was made before Teresa's team could do anything.

The coach blew his whistle and called time out. Teresa stomped over to the bench, mad and disgusted. She should've been watching Barbara. It was her fault the team had lost the ball.

At the bench, Margarita grabbed a towel and wiped her dark skin. "I'm going to kill that b . . ."

"Cool it," Keesha interrupted the string of swear words Margarita was about to utter.

"That goal was ours, *que no*?" Margarita turned to Teresa for support. "Did she push you?"

Teresa hesitated. Barbara hadn't touched her. She had grabbed the ball fair and square. However, if her teammates thought Barbara had, they wouldn't blame her for losing the play.

Teresa shrugged. "It happened so fast." It wasn't exactly a lie, but she hadn't denied Barbara's guilt either.

Margarita wouldn't let it slide.

"She did push her. I saw her," Margarita insisted angrily.

"Are you sure?" Keesha asked.

Teresa studied the black girl and tried to gauge how much Keesha had actually seen. Barbara was always showing off and acting superior. Just because she was white she thought she was hot stuff. Keesha didn't like Barbara any more than she or Margarita did, but Teresa doubted that Keesha would lie about the play.

Teresa started to protest and tell the truth, but before she had a chance, Margarita spoke out.

"She'd better stay away from me. If she comes near I'll give her a taste of her own medicine."

"Keep the game clean," Keesha warned. "We'll win and we'll do it fair."

Coach blew the whistle and Keesha returned to the field. Teresa started to follow, but Margarita grabbed her arm and held her back.

"You watch for a chance to get that witch. If she gets between us, you angle her my way."

Teresa glanced around to make sure they couldn't be heard. "She didn't touch me."

Margarita stopped mid-stride and turned to Teresa. "What do you mean? Are you going to tell and call me a liar?"

"No," Teresa quickly assured Margarita. "I just don't want any trouble."

"It's self-defense." Margarita started toward the field. "It's a matter of getting them before they get you."

"*Them*? What are you talking about?"

"*Gringas*, of course. You know they treat us like dirt."

Teresa didn't know any such thing. Whites rarely came into the barrio, and Teresa never went out of it. The only whites she knew were her teachers, and she liked them—well, maybe not Miss Barlow.

Margarita continued talking. "Just watch. She won't take the ball from me again."

Teresa sighed but kept silent. Barbara hadn't even taken the ball away from Margarita. It should have been Teresa's, but Barbara's play had been good strategy. It wouldn't do any good to point that out to her friend. Margarita was too full of hatred. Teresa didn't want that hate directed at her. She'd try to stay away from Barbara.

The game progressed and Teresa's team scored two goals, but the other team scored three. They were ahead, and there wasn't much time left. Teresa's team had better make another goal soon, or they would lose their first-place standing in the league.

The ball went out of bounds, and Teresa was selected to kick it in. She glanced around the field. Keesha and Margarita were angling into position, but every time Teresa aimed to kick, Barbara moved to block it.

Margarita hollered.

Barbara turned for a second, giving Teresa her chance. She kicked the ball to Keesha. It was not in play. Several players ran toward the goal. Keesha passed the ball back to Teresa, who dribbled it four yards and then started to pass it to Margarita.

Barbara came from nowhere to intercept the pass, but before she could get the ball Margarita ran toward her. The girls collided, but Margarita was quickly on her feet with possession of the ball.

Excited now and sure of another goal, Teresa started to follow until she heard a cry from behind her. She glanced back and saw Keesha running toward a crumpled body. Barbara.

Teresa stopped.

Margarita shouted, "Get down here. Now's our chance."

Several players were gathered around Barbara. Teresa didn't want to betray her friend, but she needed to know what had happened to Barbara.

Teresa circled in an arc and jogged toward the gathering. The coach was running also, but he was clear at the other end of the field.

When Teresa saw Barbara, she gasped. Blood oozed from her forehead. She looked unconscious.

"Who's got a handkerchief or bandanna?" someone shouted.

Teresa reached in her pocket and pulled out a turquoise cotton scarf. "I've got this. It's clean."

"Try to stop the bleeding," Keesha ordered.

Repulsed, Teresa backed up. "No way. I'm not touching her."

Keesha glared in disgust before grabbing the cloth out of Teresa's hand. "Give it to me. I'll help her."

"You're going to be in trouble," one of the other black teammates advised. "Don't be touching no white girl."

Keesha ignored the advice, and Teresa watched as Keesha applied first aid. By the time the coach arrived, the bleeding had stopped. Barbara moaned and opened her eyes. She looked confused and in pain.

Teresa glanced over at Margarita, who winked and grinned. Teresa gasped. Her friend had injured Barbara on purpose. A feeling of shame and remorse washed through her.

"Someone help me," Coach hollered. "We'll make a stretcher and get her to the office."

Teresa was the first to volunteer.

Let's look at the attitudes in this scene. What did Margarita express? Margarita's hatred was based on jealousy. She perceived whites as having more than she did, and she hated them because of it.

Is her hatred based on fact? Are all whites well off? Of course not. What Margarita didn't know was that Barbara's family were homeless and had barely survived until a local church had taken them in and helped Barbara's mother find a job. So how did Margarita come up with her attitude toward Barbara?

She could have developed the hatred in many ways. Perhaps her family hated whites and had taught her to do so. Perhaps she lived in a middle-class neighborhood where all the white children had more material things. Perhaps she wants material wealth so badly that it makes her miserable with envy.

Is Margarita happy? Would you want to experience life as she does?

Not all of the girls on the team treated Barbara badly. What was Keesha's reaction to Barbara, and how did she help the situation? If Keesha had not been kind, there may have been no one there with the courage to help Barbara. Keesha did not pay attention to envy, hatred, or fear, but acted on her instincts of gentleness and compassion to assist another human who was in need.

Do you think Keesha is torn up inside with feelings of turmoil? It is more likely that she has a sense of peace and contentment because she knows she helped another.

Keesha's attitude helped other people besides Barbara. Can you see how?

What about Teresa? She does not feel Margarita's envy or hatred. She didn't feel the one black girl's fear. She was repulsed by the blood and the idea of touching someone *different*. That is normal. Teresa was not sure how to react. Whose example did she follow?

Our behavior sets the tone not only for ourselves but for those around us. Teresa almost followed Margarita's example of prejudiced behavior. Margarita's hatred affected not just Barbara but all of the team.

Hatred turns people ugly. Margarita's attitude caused her to injure another human being. Hatred also eats away inside of you and can develop attitudes that are harmful to your health. It has been medically proved that many illnesses are the result of this disharmony of spirit. Anger, bitterness, and envy act like bile and eat away at your nervous and physical system.

Let's look at Aaron and Julia, who are at the beach in a lakeside summer resort.

Julia waited while Aaron spread his towel on the sand and then helped with hers. The sun glistened on the calm lake. It was perfect weather for tanning.

Julia stretched out on her stomach and propped her chin on her fist. It was a good position for looking around without anyone's noticing. Maybe some of her friends would show up.

"This is a great beach," Aaron said. "You're lucky you can come here every summer."

"Wait until you meet my friends." *And wait until they see you*, she thought. He was one good-looking guy. "We always come to the beach. It's where the action is."

He stretched out and rolled onto his side so that he could stare at her. Julia didn't mind. She liked his admiring glances.

"I like that swimsuit." He traced his finger along the strap of the hot pink bikini. "It shows off your figure."

Julia blushed with pleasure.

"Do you want to go in for a swim?" Aaron asked. "I'll race you to the water."

With the challenge issued, Julia jumped up and started across the sand toward the lake. Aaron was faster. He passed her up before she was halfway there.

At the water's edge, she paused to admire the motion of his body as it moved easily in the water. She really liked Aaron and hoped their relationship would grow.

"Come on in," he shouted.

She waded ankle-deep and stopped. It always surprised her how cold the water was. The icy shock brought a flood of memories of other summer trips to the lake.

Aaron started splashing. "Come on, chicken. If you don't get in here I'll come get you."

Being chased by Aaron was tempting. She glanced around the beach and saw that several more people had arrived. That kind of adventure could wait until later this evening, when they could be on the beach alone. Quickly she dove into the water. The icy chill took her breath until she started moving toward Aaron.

For an hour they swam in the crystal clear water. She took him to the point where they could climb on a pile of granite rocks and look at the tree-lined shore. They even saw a couple of fish. After they swam back, Julia said she needed some rest and persuaded Aaron to return with her to the beach.

The sand burned their feet as they walked across the beach. Aaron started to run.

"Race you."

Julia laughed and started after him.

"I won." He dove for his towel.

Julia landed on top of him. "You rat. That wasn't fair. You had a head start."

Laughing, he rolled over so that Julia ended up beside him. She brushed drops of water off his shoulders. He was so strong and attractive. She liked his smile and wished he would kiss her.

Laughter sounded behind her, but she paid little attention to it. She was staring into Aaron's blue eyes.

Someone shouted from behind them. "*Venga mi hija.*"

The Spanish words acted like a blow. Julia sat up straight. She didn't want to look, afraid of what she'd see. Slowly she turned around. Sure enough, a Mexican family were putting out their blanket only yards from her and Aaron. A toddler was running toward the water, and an older brother was chasing her.

"Oh, no." Julia felt a sick feeling growing inside of her. "Not here. Why did *they* have to show up?"

"What's the matter? Do you know those people?" Aaron asked.

"No, I don't know them." Anger made her restless. She turned to Aaron. "That's the problem. They don't belong here."

Concern showed in Aaron's expression. "What do you mean? I thought this was a public beach."

"They're from Mexico," she bit out as hatred churned inside. "They come here illegally to work in the clubs."

"So? They probably work for low wages. Americans won't take those jobs."

"They're pigs. They come here and trash up the whole place."

"They probably don't have..."

Julia interrupted him. "Why are you defending them? I'm embarrassed you had to see this. At first they hardly ever came to the beach. Then last year it started getting really bad." She gestured toward the family. The more she looked at them, the angrier she became, and that made her voice get louder. "Now, look. They're all over the place," she practically shouted.

"Shh. They'll hear you." Aaron motioned for her to quiet down. That only made her madder.

"It doesn't matter. They don't understand English. They don't even bother to learn it." Her stomach started to burn, as it always did when she became upset. "Just listen to them. Don't you hate it when they rattle on like that?"

Julia held her stomach; it had started to hurt so much. "I hate it when all these Mexicans come here. They're taking over the place."

Aaron started gathering his belongings. Good. She wanted to go find a beach that didn't have all this trash on it.

"There's another beach about two miles from here," she started to explain.

"Is that right?" Aaron's voice sounded tight and strained.

Julia looked into his face and saw disappointment and anger.

"You go on to whatever beach you want," he told her. "I'm going back to the city."

Stunned, Julia stared. "What are you talking about? They aren't everywhere. We can . . ."

He interrupted her. "You don't understand, Julia. I just found out that I don't want to be around you anymore."

If he had slapped her, she wouldn't have been more shocked. "What . . . what are you saying?"

Aaron had started to walk away, but he stopped and turned to her. His blue eyes looked like chips of ice. "My cousins are Mexicans, Julia. Since you don't want to be around them, I guess that would apply to me as well. *Adios*."

Sharp pain knifed through Julia as she watched Aaron disappear from sight.

Julia was obviously filled with prejudice that had developed into hatred. What purpose did it serve her? What harm did it cause? Who suffered the most from her behavior? Certainly not the Mexican family. They probably sensed her antagonism, but they weren't hurt by her words since they didn't understand them.

How do you think Aaron feels now that we know of his family? He's probably hurt and surely regrets his relationship with Julia.

These responses do not compare at all to what Julia suffered from her behavior. Not only did she lose her boyfriend, but she's left with anger and bitterness churning within her. These emotions do more damage to the person who has them than to the recipient.

Julia is suffering from an ulcer. Nerves, tension, and worry cause ulcers. Can you see how Julia is damaging herself? What alternatives does she have? How can she get rid of her negative thoughts and become happy and healthy again?

Hatred and anger are not the only negative feelings that damage our lives. Envy and poor choices do an equally good job of it. Ken goes to a high school with a large Jewish population. Art has just moved to the school and doesn't realize that it's Rosh Hashanah, the Jewish New Year.

Art strolled into class and stared at all the empty seats. He glanced at the clock to see if he was early. Maybe he had set his watch wrong this morning.

The clock struck nine and the bell rang. Shaking his head, Art sat next to Ken.

"What's going on?" He glanced around again, disappointed that Anne wasn't there. She was a knockout and always had a smile for him. "Where's everyone?"

Ken stared at him as if he thought he was nuts. Art shifted uncomfortably in his seat and shrugged. Hey, he didn't know.

"You new here?" Ken asked.

"Yeah. Moved from San Diego three weeks ago."

Just then Miss Rowe finished taking attendance and stood up. Class was about to begin.

"I'll explain it later," Ken whispered.

Art nodded and prepared to take notes. To his surprise, Miss Rowe didn't lecture.

"Since there are so many absences, we'll skip today's lesson," she told the class.

Everyone in class cheered.

She smiled. "You have your term paper subjects. I'll let you work on them this period."

Art couldn't believe it. No lecture today. What luck. He hadn't finished the homework. This break would give him a chance to catch up.

The hour passed quickly. Not only did Art finish last night's assignment, he finished them for the whole week. That would give him time to go to the library in the evening and work on his term paper.

When the bell rang, Ken motioned for Art to follow him. Together they strolled down the hall. Its emptiness was eerie.

"What's up? Is there an epidemic?" Art asked.

"No way. It's some Jewish holiday."

Surprised, Art stopped walking. Ken noticed and backed up until they were even.

"All those students are Jewish?" Art immediately thought of Anne.

"We're in their neighborhood." Ken shrugged. "Didn't you know that?"

"Obviously not."

"Well, no matter. You'll learn." Bitterness sounded in his voice. "They've got more holidays."

"And the school empties out like this?"

"Right, and I'm splitting next. I'm not hanging around here. If they get the day off, so do I."

"The school allows it?"

"No way." Ken chuckled. "The trick is to come to first-period class for your attendance and then cut out to the beach. The surf's up."

"You mean ditch classes?" Art asked, surprised.

"Why not? With so many absent they never teach anything. Who's gonna miss us?"

"Does everyone do like Miss Rowe and give you study time?"

"Everyone but Baker. He always throws a party." Ken turned the corner and headed toward the exit. Art followed close beside him, pumping him for more answers.

At the door, Ken paused. "How about it? Want to come to the beach? A bunch of us are leaving right now."

Art debated for a few seconds. The beach did appeal. There was good surfing near the pier just a mile away. Then he thought about his calculus and chemistry classes. If the teachers weren't busy he could ask them about those two chapters he had trouble with. It might make a difference on his final grade.

"I think I'll stick around," Art said. "Maybe I'll come by after school."

"It's your funeral, pal." Ken opened the door and left.

What cultural differences did Art face? Ken's reaction was envy. He didn't like the idea that half the student body had the day off, never mind that these students were involved in religious activities, not a day at the beach. What purpose did cutting school and going to the beach serve Ken? Do you think it's a subtle form of revenge? How does his reaction to envy harm him?

Art didn't react in the same manner. He was envious of

the students who weren't in school, but he didn't let the feeling rule his reason.

Everyone is master of his or her actions and reactions. You can put ten students in the exact same situation and they will respond in ten different ways. What you must decide is how you want to live.

If anger, hatred, envy, and malice rule your life, you will act and react in negative and harmful ways. Margarita's overt actions created negative behavior. Julia's hate not only caused external problems such as the loss of her boyfriend, but internal problems as well. She is hurting her body with tension and ulcers. External and internal reactions both cause *you* the most damage.

Positive reactions give you more peace. In the next chapter we shall see what a simple act of kindness can accomplish.

CHAPTER ◇ 7

What an Act of Kindness Can Do

If your reactions determine the type of life you lead, it is important to consider the results of your actions. In the last chapter, Margarita reacted negatively to her feelings of envy and hatred. She caused bodily harm to Barbara, she tried to make Teresa act as an accomplice, and she generally projected an attitude of hate.

Our behavior sets the tone not only for ourselves but for those around us. Because Margarita projected hate, the girls did not want to help Barbara. They were influenced by Margarita's attitude.

If Keesha had not come along and shown compassion, do you think Teresa would have had the courage on her own to be helpful? Keesha's one act of thoughtfulness defused Margarita's hatred. It acted to spur the other girls into showing kindness also.

Multicultural interaction can sometimes be unpleasant.

We've seen examples that were mean and nasty, yet kindness salvaged some of them. Remember Mr. Stewart, the black man in the mall. He chose kindness instead of revenge. Remember Seth Yoder? His religion dictated that he remain gentle. Chad showed consideration for Steve's financial situation.

In all of those situations the teens had a choice. They decided whether they would act in a positive or negative manner. In every incident the situation could have changed, given a different reaction.

That is important to understand. *You* determine the events in your life. How you decide to react affects not only you but those around you.

Let's look at some situations and see what an act of kindness does.

Marlena glanced around the crowded family room and smiled. Her party was a success. There was always someone at the buffet table. Everyone had complimented her on the punch. Most of her friends were mingling, and several couples were dancing.

All afternoon she had been a nervous wreck. Getting everything ready was part of it, but mainly she had worried that no one would show up. There were tons of people. She could relax now and enjoy herself. Except for one thing.

Marlena glanced over to the corner where Lon stood alone. She had tried to get her involved in several conversations, but as soon as Marlena would leave, Lon would return to the corner. Of course, it didn't help that Lon spoke no English.

"What's wrong, Sis? You look down in the dumps."

At the sound of her brother's voice, a rush of joy ran

through Marlena, making her forget her worry over Lon. "Jerry, you came!"

"Said I would, didn't I?" He tweaked her chin affectionately.

Her party would really be a winner now. Jerry was the most popular senior at school. She knew for a fact that most of the girls in the room had come hoping to see him.

"Thanks for showing up," she told him.

"Nothing I wouldn't do for my little sis." He jiggled his eyebrows like a clown.

Marlena chuckled and then sobered. "Are you serious about helping?"

Jerry hesitated, obviously not wanting to commit himself too far. He had a date for later that evening. Marlena quickly reassured him.

"It's no big thing, but see that girl over there? The one with the long black hair. She's Vietnamese."

"Sure. What's the matter?"

"I don't know what to do with her. She doesn't speak English, and she just stands in that corner like a statue. I wish I hadn't invited her."

"Hey, what kind of talk is that? She's probably just scared."

"I don't think so."

Jerry rubbed his jaw, a sign that he was thinking. "Maybe she doesn't know how to act at a party."

"That's obvious, isn't it?" She let Jerry hear the sarcasm in her voice.

"Don't be snide. She's been brought up in another country. How would she know what to do at an American party?"

"And how am I supposed to tell her if she can't talk to me?"

"She's learning by watching. You might let her be."

"I suppose," Marlena conceded. "But she looks so forlorn standing all alone."

Jerry popped the last of the peanuts he'd been eating into his mouth. "Leave it to me, sis. I'll take care of it."

Giving her a teasing grin, he worked his way through the crowd toward Lon. Marlena noticed how all of her friends greeted him as he passed by. She also saw how they stared after him. She shook her head. That brother of hers was something else.

It took close to fifteen minutes and several stops to visit before Jerry reached the Vietnamese girl. Marlena worked her way in the same direction, deciding it might be a good idea to stay close in case Jerry upset Lon. Most girls loved his attention, but Lon was different.

By the time Marlena got close enough to hear part of the conversation, Jerry was showing Lon how to dance.

"See, you take a step this way." He started to shake his hips. "And wiggle a little that way."

Lon covered her mouth with her fingers and giggled. Marlena tapped her foot, wondering what had come over her brother.

Another number began, and Jerry grabbed Lon's hand. "Come on. We'll try it out here."

Lon was reluctant to follow Jerry to the cleared space where everyone was dancing. He just laughed and didn't give her much choice.

At first she froze, not knowing what to do, but soon Jerry had everyone around them involved in showing her the basic steps. By the time the next record started, Lon was dancing. Jerry stayed with her through two more numbers and then handed her over to a friend of Marlena's.

Marlena waved a hand to catch Jerry's attention. Puffing from the exercise, he stood in front of her.

"You know what the problem was, don't you?"

"I have a pretty good idea."

"She was afraid someone was going to ask her to dance, and she didn't know how."

"That must be why she didn't want to talk to anyone," Marlena guessed.

"That would be my bet." Jerry patted her cheek. "Look, Sis. It's been fun. I've got to go. Big date."

She stood on tiptoes and stretched to give her brother a kiss on the cheek.

"Thanks, Jerry. You're the best."

After she watched Jerry leave, Marlena turned back to see how Lon was doing. Half expecting her to be back in the corner, she was surprised to see her dancing with someone else.

Marlena smiled. Lon was on her way to popularity.

Jerry didn't do very much. It took only a few minutes of his time to help out with Lon. But those few moments will have a lifelong effect on the girl.

Coming to a country that has such strange customs takes a lot of bravery and guts. Nevertheless, uncertainties are plentiful. Lon preferred to stand alone rather than risk looking foolish in front of her new friends.

Jerry's act of kindness not only opened Lon up so that she could be more receptive to change, it also affected the others around them.

Lon had sent body-language messages that said leave me alone. Other students may have wanted to include Lon in their conversations, but seeing her standing so stiff and alone didn't encourage them to try.

Jerry set an example for the others. He broke the ice. Several teens are asking Lon to dance. Now that she knows how, she's not afraid to do so in front of the others.

One small act can accomplish much. Let's see another example where kindness influences others. Sophie has just volunteered to work on the Homecoming Dance planning committee. The first meeting is running late.

Sophie brushed back her dark curls and stretched her back. She had been sitting in this hard wooden chair for hours, and her body was beginning to rebel.

A quick glance at the clock showed that it was already past six. Ma was going to kill her if she didn't get home.

"What do you think of that idea, Sophie?" Jesse asked.

The question caught her off guard. She blushed. "Sorry. I didn't hear it."

Jesse frowned, and Sophie's heart sank. She didn't want the popular junior annoyed with her.

"I guess my mind wandered for a minute," she apologized. "Can you repeat your question?"

Amy put down her pencil and spoke before Jesse could respond. "We're all getting rummy. We've been working on this for hours."

Jesse glanced at his watch. "How did it get so late?" he asked.

"We've accomplished a lot," Raquel pointed out. "Let's break for now. We can finish up next week."

Jesse agreed. Everyone began packing up their notes as he set a time for their next meeting.

"Same time, same place," he said.

"Wednesday's fine with me," Amy added as she stood and brushed back her long ponytail. For a brief second Sophie envied Amy's tall slim figure and straight blonde hair. Sophie had inherited her grandmother's short rounded body and natural dark curls. Her last boyfriend had liked her curves. She wondered if Jesse did too or if he preferred the long leggy type.

Chairs scraped across the hardwood floors as the others stood. The noise distracted Sophie from her thoughts. Quickly she got up too.

Outside the sun had set, and it was dark. A brief uneasiness came as she thought about walking home alone. Raquel lived nearby. Maybe she could walk part way with her.

"Are you walking, Raquel?" she asked.

"Yes. Shall we walk together?" Raquel seemed as relieved as she felt.

"We can make it most of the way together if we cut through the park."

"Hey, you two aren't walking alone?" Jesse joined them. "It's dark out there. I wouldn't advise it."

"I can call my brother to come get us," Raquel suggested. "He works at the drugstore. He could pick us up on the way to one of his deliveries."

"Don't bother him," Jesse told them. "I'm taking Amy home. Come on with us. I'll drop you two off also. There's plenty of room in my car."

Raquel accepted immediately, and since she and Amy had, Sophie didn't mind doing so also.

"Thanks, Jesse. My mother's going to be upset as it is with my being so late. A ride will get me home that much sooner."

"We'll drop you off first then." Jesse's smile melted her heart.

Sophie had a feeling she was falling in love. The feeling grew stronger as she followed the handsome junior to his car. When she saw the car, she knew for sure.

"That's a mean-looking Trans Am," she exclaimed.

"We get to ride in that?" Raquel practically jumped for joy.

"You and Amy get in the back," he told her. "Sophie, since you're going to be first out, you sit up front with me."

Gladly, she thought. Now she wished she was going to be last. Even if it meant sitting in the back seat now. She knew the others would have their turns up front. Imagine spending all that time with Jesse.

Everyone piled in, and Jesse started the powerful engine. A red light beeped over Sophie's head, and she asked what it was.

"It's a monitor for radar. Let's me know when the cops are checking for speeding."

Evidently none were around, because Jesse was going fast. He had perfect control, though. Sophie had to admire the way he maneuvered the corners as he left the school grounds.

"Where to?" Jesse asked as he came to the main intersection.

The question caught Sophie up short. For the first time she realized that by accepting Jesse's invitation she would have to tell him where she lived. She shifted uncomfortably in the plush seat. Jesse obviously had money. What would he think of her run-down Italian neighborhood? It wasn't poverty level or anything that bad. It was just old and kind of dingy. Jesse probably lived uptown in one of those classy neighborhoods. Maybe she'd better walk after all.

Evidently Sophie had waited too long, and Raquel began to give directions. Jesse nosed the car to the right and headed toward the park. It was too late now.

"You know, if these meetings are going to run this late,

why don't we just plan on my taking you home from each one."

"That's great," Raquel accepted the offer. "We appreciate it, and I know my folks will be happier. They worry when it gets this late."

Jesse's offer was more than generous. Sophie sighed. He'd have to see her house sometime. The fall evenings were not only going to be dark, but chilly as well.

"I can understand that," Jesse commented as he turned down a dark narrow street. "Maybe I'd better come in and introduce myself to your folks. That way they won't worry so much."

"Oh, no. You don't need to do that," Sophie said quickly.

The panic must have sounded in her voice, because Jesse turned and stared for a brief moment before turning his attention back to his driving.

"No problem," Jesse assured her. "It will only take a minute for you and Raquel. I've already met Amy's folks."

"That's right." Amy spoke up. "They really were glad too. Now they don't worry if I'm late."

Sophie groaned inwardly. How was she going to get out of this? What they said was true. Her parents would want to meet Jesse, but she didn't want him meeting them.

They were so old-fashioned, especially Nonna. Her grandmother had arrived from Italy as an older woman, and she hadn't changed one bit. Inside her house, you stepped back in time. It was really Old Country. You might as well be smack dab in the middle of Italy.

Raquel continued giving directions, and Jesse pulled up in front of the narrow brick building. Usually the sight of home brought a sense of security. Not tonight. Jesse opened the door and was out and opening hers before she could protest again.

The smells of oregano and tomato filled the air as they

walked up the steps. Maybe Nonna would be in the kitchen cooking and Jesse wouldn't see her.

Light shone through the beveled glass as Sophie unlocked the door. It was warm inside and welcoming, but she didn't notice that. Instead she saw for the first time how threadbare the Persian carpet was. The clutter of glass figurines and crocheted lace on the hall tables looked old-fashioned and quaint.

"My folks are in here." She guided him toward the parlor and introduced her father and mother.

"We appreciate your driving Sophie home." Her father shook Jesse's hand.

A flutter of movement distracted Jesse. Sophie looked up in time to see her grandmother come through the door. Her lined face broke into a smile. "There you are, child. Dinner's been waiting."

Sophie tried to smile back, but all she could do was stare at the clumpy black shoes with the thick heels, the plain black dress, and the old-fashioned shawl on her grandmother's frail shoulders. What was Jesse going to think?

Jesse stepped past Sophie and extended his hand. "I'm afraid it's my fault, ma'am. I kept Sophie at a meeting." He smiled and bowed slightly. "Sure smells good. If I'd known she was missing this, I'd have adjourned the meeting pronto."

"My, my." Nonna smiled. "Such a charming young man. No wonder you were late, child."

"Nonna," Sophie whispered.

"Can you stay for supper?" Sophie's Mom asked. "We have plenty."

"No. I'd better hustle out that door."

"He still has to take Raquel and Amy home," Sophie explained as she guided Jesse toward the entranceway.

Before he stepped outside, he stopped and winked.

"Great family. Next time I'll drop you off last. That sauce smells like it was made in heaven."

"Seriously?" Sophie asked. This wasn't real. Or was it? His smile disappeared. "That is, if you don't mind."

Was he nuts, she thought. "I'd love to have you stay."

He waved good-bye and returned to the car. Sophie shut the door and danced back into the house.

Sophie was clearly embarrassed by the cultural differences of her family. She felt vulnerable and afraid that Jess might not approve. She may have felt that he would hurt her relatives' feelings, and after all, they were her family and she loved them.

How did Jesse react, and how do you suppose that made Sophie's family feel? What if he had reacted as Sophie had feared? Think of the damage he would have caused Nonna, Sophie's parents, and Sophie herself.

Many second- and third-generation teens face this problem. Their family still lives with many of the cultural traits of the Old World. Often they speak their native language. Teens who are born and raised in the United States confront two worlds when they are old enough to go to school—one culture at home, another on the outside. Usually they don't match, and conflicts occur. Do you act as your family wants, or do you try to fit in with your friends? It is a very real dilemma.

Jesse's act of kindness assured Sophie that he accepted both of her worlds. She did not have to choose between them to please him. You can see how that would ease the pressure on Sophie.

Sometimes an act of kindness means the difference between life and death. Let's find out what happened to

Felipe one Friday night when he and his friends were cruising Central Avenue in his low-rider.

A pair of fuzzy dice bobbed from the rear-view mirror as Felipe bounced the rear end of his low-rider. Miguel and Ricardo were in the back, laughing and whistling. Mingo sat beside him, his teeth white against his dark-skinned face.

"*Aaiii*," Mingo shouted. "Make it go up again, man."

"Once more," Miguel shouted. "That's so cool."

"Forget it." Felipe sounded as disappointed as he felt. "The battery's getting low. We've got to cruise some more."

"Then we'll be back, *qué no*?" Ricardo asked.

Felipe shrugged. "Maybe."

The car lowered until it was barely off the ground. Felipe pressed the gas pedal, and the car shot forward.

"Let's check out the action. I thought I saw Rita go by."

Everyone agreed quickly. Felipe laughed. He loved cruising down Central. The street was packed. There were plenty of low-riders, their windows lined with dangling balls. Music blasted from every vehicle, including theirs.

"Hey you, move over!"

Felipe and his friends peered out to see who was yelling at them. All they saw were huge tires. Felipe gripped the wheel. He could guess who they belonged to. "Hold your ground, *Ese*," Mingo advised. "It's just that jerk Ryan. Thinks he's hot stuff with that four-by-four."

Ryan's truck edged closer to the car. Felipe gripped the wheel and kept his hold steady. No redneck was going to push him off the road.

Miguel and Mingo were hurling insults out the window.

Felipe wished they'd leave the jerk alone. He didn't want his new paint job scratched just because some idiot got mad and careless.

Suddenly the car ahead stopped. Felipe slammed on the brakes, sending his friends lurching forward. An aluminum can bounced off his hood and Ryan shot ahead, his K.C.s reflecting in the city lights.

"Did you see what he did?" Mingo shouted.

Miguel and Ricardo swore in the back. Felipe was upset, but not that much. The can hadn't dinged the paint, and to be honest he was glad that Ryan was gone. He didn't trust the troublemaker.

"Look, there's Rita." Mingo pointed to the third lane over.

That made all four boys forget the incident with Ryan. They wanted to see who was in the car with Rita.

Mingo whistled out the open window. Felipe brushed back his straight black hair, hoping she'd notice that he'd had it styled. One of these days it would be Rita in the car, not his friends.

The light turned green, and Rita's Cutlass shot ahead. Felipe was still behind the turkey in the converted VW. Couldn't he go faster?

By the time Felipe crossed the intersection he had lost Rita. He didn't see her again, nor Ryan, until a couple of hours later when they were on their way home. Traffic had eased, and he could see Rita's Cutlass waiting at the stoplight. Felipe pressed the gas pedal as his friends cheered.

Just as he was about to catch up with Rita, Ryan's truck veered on the other side of him. Felipe's heart sank. Miguel swore.

"Don't let him take us," Mingo advised. "If he cuts in front of you we'll never catch up to Rita."

"Don't worry. I've got everything under control," Felipe assured them.

Just then blinking yellow lights appeared in front of them. "Road construction ahead," he told his friends. "Get ready. Ryan's going to go for it."

From his open window, he could hear Ryan revving up the truck. Felipe shifted gears. The blinking yellow lights formed an arrow warning of the closed lane ahead.

Ryan sped forward. Felipe kept even with him.

"Don't let him in," Ricardo shouted.

"Let him burn," Miguel agreed.

They were reaching the end of the warning zone. Only a few feet were left. Felipe gunned his motor until suddenly he saw the construction workers near the lights. Ryan wasn't going to make it. Felipe didn't know if Ryan had seen the men. The idiot wasn't braking. He'd never stop in time.

Felipe slammed on his brakes and let Ryan squeeze in front of him. Fortunately there was no one behind him. As he passed the crew he saw the fright on their faces, but they were all okay.

"What did you do that for?" Miguel demanded to know. "We owed those jerks."

"Shut up," Ricardo muttered. He sounded in about the same shape Felipe was in. "Felipe just saved those men's lives."

"What men? What are you talking about?"

He gripped the wheel so no one would see how his hands were shaking while Ricardo told Mingo and Miguel what had happened.

Felipe appeared to have chickened out in the clash between the two cars. Fortunately, Felipe did not chicken out but showed courage with his quick decision to let Ryan's truck change lanes.

If Felipe had not bent a little and given in, what were the possible consequences? Ricardo had seen the men too, and he explained to Miguel and Mingo, but what if he hadn't seen? Felipe would have had to face the resentment of his friends.

Acting with compassion and keeping your head is not always easy, especially when dealing with situations of cultural differences. Felipe showed extreme courage in risking the esteem of his peers to possibly save a life.

Imagine how Felipe would have felt if he hadn't put on the brakes and one of the workers had been killed. Would he want to live with that kind of guilt for the rest of his life? That worker could have been the father of a friend or perhaps an uncle or cousin.

It is tempting to become angry when we feel we've been insulted. Keeping control of your reactions and emotions could save your life. It will certainly make it more pleasant and peaceful.

CHAPTER ◇ 8

How Patience Affects Interaction

We have seen how compassion and kindness have a positive effect on multicultural interaction. Patience is also an important ingredient of successful relationships.

In the last chapter, we saw how many generations it took for Sophie's family to become Americanized. Nonna, the grandmother, will probably never be completely American. Picture yourself moving to another country and you'll understand why. Even if you moved there because you wanted to, you'll never forget the childhood memories of your native land.

This experience is the same for everyone. Students who come to the United States from a foreign country bring their culture, language, and feelings with them.

It is important to remember that most people come to our country because they want to. This desire gives them the motivation to become Americanized, at least in public.

If these people stay in the United States, they make sure that their children conform to American society. Statistics prove this to be true. You saw that Sophie of the third generation is completely Americanized.

What does this mean? We need to have patience in dealing with people from other countries. They will seem strange, sound funny, eat different foods, but there is no real threat that one group of foreigners will change America. The case has always been that the foreigners *become* American.

The problem for us is how to deal with these people until that happens. Patience is the key.

Let's meet Prem. He has just arrived from India, and Burt and Derek have invited him over on Saturday. They both live at the lake and have jet skis, which they are trying to teach Prem to use.

Derek opened the throttle and tore across the still water of the lake. Power throbbed beneath him, forcing him to bend his knees and absorb the jolts as the jet ski bounced across the water.

Wind blew his hair back and chilled his wet skin. Derek didn't even feel the cold. He was too charged up with the excitement of speed and danger.

The engine roared as he leaned into a turn. Water sparkled below him as he took the curve at top speed. He was leaning so far over he could have reached down and touched the water.

For ten minutes he skied, staying near shore so Prem could see what he was doing. He'd have to go in soon so the Indian could try it. Derek and Burt had spent the whole morning teaching him the names of the important parts. Prem could point to the controls and knew how they worked. Now came the test to see if he could put it all together in action.

Derek headed in. Waves backwashed over him as he released the throttle and the craft came to a halt. Derek stepped off and balanced the machine.

"Okay," he hollered to Burt. "Bring him over and let's try this baby out."

Prem followed Burt, an ear-to-ear grin on his face. "I ready," he said, his words heavily accented.

Derek laughed. "You bet you are. Now listen close."

Slowly, Derek pointed to the parts to remind Prem of their names. Then he began to explain how to operate the ski.

At first Prem did well in understanding the basic steps, but halfway through the lesson he bogged down. Derek tried to explain but couldn't seem to get across that Prem had to move before he could get balanced.

Frustrated, Derek looked at Burt. "What am I doing wrong?" he asked his friend. "Can you explain it better?"

Burt nodded and took hold of the handlebars. Slowly he repeated key words and phrases. As he did, he demonstrated each step.

Prem nodded and smiled and, to Derek's relief, seemed to be understanding what he had to do.

"Think he's ready to try it?" Derek asked.

"Only one way to find out," Burt said.

"Here goes, then."

Derek went through it one more time before stepping back. Prem climbed onto the jet ski and promptly rolled it over. Derek bit his tongue so as not to laugh.

Again Prem climbed onto the ski. This time he stayed upright. Carefully he gripped the bars, but he turned the throttle too fast. Like a caged animal, the engine roared and the jet ski bolted. Prem landed in the water.

Three times Prem did the same thing. It was no longer comical. It was getting downright annoying.

"No, no, no." Derek waded toward Prem. The water was above his chest so he couldn't go fast.

Prem helped Derek push the craft closer to shore where the water wasn't so deep.

"Now, listen," Derek said. "You grab the bars like this and you turn the throttle slowly."

By the time he had finished the sentence he was shouting. Prem's expression was closed, but anger glittered in his dark eyes. He turned around and started toward the beach.

"Wait a minute." Burt grabbed Prem's arm. "It's all right."

Prem stood unmoving and not looking at Derek.

"You don't need to shout, Derek. He can't speak English. That doesn't mean he's deaf."

"I give up." Derek raised his hands in a gesture of defeat. "You teach him. He listens to you."

Derek handed the jet ski over to Burt and stepped back. Burt began explaining to Prem. As he did so he covered Prem's hand with his own so that he could show him how to turn the throttle.

Prem seemed to be taking it in, but Burt was going so slow that they would be here all afternoon before Prem got on the thing. He might as well go back to the beach and get a soda out of the cooler. This was going to take all day.

Derek waded in to shore. The sand was hot now, so he ran to the towels and quickly stretched out. Melted ice dripped from the can as he popped the aluminum and took a swallow.

Suddenly a roar from the ski's engine cut into the silence. Derek stared in disbelief. Prem was on the ski and moving.

Burt joined him on shore as soon as he saw that Prem had the hang of it.

"How'd you manage that?" Derek asked.

"Patience, my man. You've got to be patient."

Often a person who knows only one language makes the mistake of shouting when speaking to a foreigner. It isn't volume that will make your words clear. It's slow, clear pronunciation.

Furthermore, as we saw with Derek, Prem, and Burt, teaching someone a second language requires patience. Not only were Burt and Derek teaching Prem how to ride a jet ski, but he was learning English at the same time. This double load of information takes time to sink in. Burt was wise to go slow with his directions to Prem.

Derek's shouting not only was unnecessary, but it also conveyed how upset he was that Prem wasn't understanding. That tension probably added to Prem's distress, making it difficult to learn. Remember that language is difficult to recall when a person is under stress.

Learning languages isn't the only time we need to exercise patience in dealing with cultural differences. Sometimes we need to be patient with ourselves. If we haven't sought the cultural interaction—for example, if it is forced on us—it is very difficult to have patience with the differences.

Take for example these students' reaction to the daughter of the new Japanese owner of the local factory. Most of the families in town resent the foreign ownership of their industry. Because of that, there is little motivation to get along with Kiyomi.

* * *

Denise took careful steps across the uneven ground so that she wouldn't drop the cake. When she got to the picnic tables she knew she was in trouble. There wasn't an empty space big enough for the large cake her mother had spent hours on last night.

"Alice!" She hollered for her younger sister. "Come help me."

She glanced around the picnic table area but didn't see a sign of her sister's carrot-top curls.

"Here, let me help," a quiet voice said.

Denise turned to see a petite Japanese girl with slanted eyes and a shy smile shoving pie tins aside to make room.

"Thanks," Denise murmured. "This is getting heavy."

She put the cake on the table and straightened up. "Look at all this food. Why, there's enough to feed an army."

She glanced at the girl who had helped her, and who seemed nervous. "Are you Mr. Matsudaira's daughter?"

Mr. Matsudaira was her Dad's new boss. Denise had heard Alice mention that his daughter was in her ninth-grade class.

The girl nodded. "My name's Kiyomi."

"I'm Denise, Alice's sister. You haven't seen her, have you? She's got curly red hair."

Kiyomi's eyes seemed to widen, as if she were surprised. Denise wondered why until Kiyomi pointed toward the baseball diamond.

"She's over there. All the kids are playing ball."

"That figures," Denise muttered. "When there's work to be done, Alice is an expert at disappearing from sight."

Kiyomi smiled.

"How come you aren't playing with them?"

The smile disappeared. Denise frowned as she considered why. Maybe Kiyomi didn't like the game, although she had heard that baseball was very popular in Japan. Still, that didn't necessarily mean anything. Baseball was popular here too, and Denise hated the game. Hurry up and wait—that's all it was to her.

"Look." Denise brushed cake crumbs from her fingers. "Would you mind going to the diamond and telling Alice to get over here. She's supposed to help unload the car."

Kiyomi backed away, shaking her head. "No, I can't do that."

Denise stared in surprise.

Kiyomi's face brightened. "Why don't I help you instead? Alice is busy. I'm not."

Denise started to protest until she saw the pleading in the girl's expression. Then she remembered the lost look she had seen earlier. Kiyomi needed something to do.

"Sure. Come along. I could really use the help."

At the car, her Mom was piling chairs from the back of the Suburban Wagon. Denise introduced Kiyomi, and together they started carrying the lawn chairs and more boxes of food.

"I love these company picnics," Denise said as they headed across the grass. "Have you been to one before?"

Kiyomi shook her head no.

"You'll love it. Everyone plays baseball or volleyball. The men toss horseshoes."

Kiyomi frowned at that.

"Don't you know what horseshoes are?"

"No. Are they part of a horse?"

Denise laughed and then explained the game. Before they went back for another load from the car, Denise walked Kiyomi past the horseshoe pits to watch for a minute.

"I bet your Dad will want to learn," she said as they returned to the car. "He should, anyway. If you want to be in here in this town, you need to know how to toss the iron."

At Kiyomi's frown, Denise chuckled again. "How long have you been here, anyway?"

"Two months."

"That explains it. Don't worry, you'll learn."

It took two more trips to finish taking picnic supplies from the car. Denise introduced Kiyomi to her Dad, who barely said hello. She didn't think much of that, knowing how busy he was. As one of the plant supervisors, he had to organize events like this picnic. Because of that, he rarely had time to really enjoy himself.

Now that her chores were done, Denise wanted to find her friends. Daryll had said he was going to play volleyball. She was sure that was where the gang was.

She started to walk toward the river where volleyball nets had been put up in the sand. A movement beside her caught her attention, and she turned to see Kiyomi. The girl looked lost again.

"Where's your family?" Denise asked.

"My Dad's talking to some men over there." She pointed to a group sitting on the grass.

"Your Mom?"

Kiyomi frowned. "She died. It's just me and my father."

"I'm sorry to hear that," Denise said with sincerity. Then she didn't know what to do. She wanted to go find her friends, but Kiyomi looked so lost.

"Come along with me," she finally decided. "We'll go find Alice and get you in that ball game."

Kiyomi's face lit up. She hurried to follow Denise.

At the baseball diamond, Denise easily spotted her sister's bright red hair. She was out in left field.

"Wait here," she told Kiyomi and jogged out to her sister.

"What did you bring *her* around for?" Alice demanded.

Denise halted in surprise. "I brought her to play ball. Why? What's wrong?"

"Thanks a lot." Alice put her hands on her hips. "Do you know how long it took us to get rid of her?"

"What are you talking about?" Denise couldn't believe she was hearing this. "What's wrong with letting her play?"

"Don't be dense. You know who her Dad is, don't you?"

"Of course. He owns the plant now."

"And everybody in town hates him."

"That's because he's a tough boss and won't let people get away with sloppy work. You've heard Dad say he's tough, but fair."

"I know," Alice said. "But most of my friends don't like him."

"So—because their fathers don't like to work hard, you're going to be mean to Kiyomi? She doesn't have anything to do with what her father does at the plant."

Alice blushed. "I know that, but the others . . ."

Denise could see that the problem was making Alice very uncomfortable. It wasn't fair to demand that her sister buck peer pressure. It would take time for the town to open up and accept these strangers.

She sighed and headed back to Kiyomi. As she saw the forlorn expression on the young girl's face, Denise made up her mind.

"They're in the middle of a game here. Come on with me. We're going to go cheer for the girls. They're playing volleyball against the guys."

Kiyomi smiled and followed Denise, who was pleased to see that Alice and her friends were taking note of Denise's friendliness toward Kiyomi. Maybe they'd follow her example later. She'd give them time.

* * *

Alice and her friends were afraid to be friendly with Kiyomi. They had no basis for their feelings, so they were being prejudiced by town gossip. Denise's act of kindness will go a long way in setting a positive example for Alice and her friends.

The true key to Denise's success, however, was not pointing out the false basis of their prejudice, nor was it demonstrating an act of kindness. Both of those things helped, but the real power she gave to all concerned was patience.

What would have happened if Denise had forced Alice and her friends to let Kiyomi play ball with them? How would Kiyomi have felt? Would it have made it easier to accept the Japanese student?

By not pressing the issue, yet not giving in to it either, Denise allowed everyone time to change their thinking. If everyone sees Kiyomi having a good time with Denise, they will be more open to the idea of including her in their activities. They will begin to see her as a normal human being instead of someone strange and foreign.

Patience is also vital when dealing with tense situations. Remember that when tension increases, things you've learned about new cultures become secondary. You rely on what you know best.

To cope with tense situations you need to develop patience. If you force yourself to remain calm and let matters fall into place, it will prove better in the long run.

Unfortunately, patience is usually the last thing we have during an emergency. East High has taken a group of students on a field trip. Bandar and his sister Anoud, both students from Saudi Arabia, are on the same bus.

* * *

Bandar sat next to his American friend, Rob, and enjoyed the chance to be quiet and think. It was so hard always to speak English. After listening to lectures all day, he had a headache.

He sighed. He'd give anything for some of the strong tea his grandmother brewed back home in the harem. There were no harems in the United States. His father had left most of the women behind while he attended the university for a year. He had brought only Bandar and Anoud and a few servants.

Bandar glanced at his sister, who sat in the front of the bus. Sometimes he wished his father had not allowed her to come. She liked the ways of the West too much. She even let the Americans call her Ann instead of using her Muslim name.

Bandar closed his eyes. At least she was not sitting next to any boys for him to worry about, and Rob was here next to him. He knew that Rob had eyes for his sister. Bandar would watch Anoud closely. He had promised his father.

Suddenly, the bus lurched. Bandar grabbed hold of the seat in front of him. Before he could brace himself properly the bus swerved off the road.

Screams echoed as it careened down the hill. Grunts and mumbled words followed when it came to a crunching halt. Looking straight ahead, Bandar saw that a wall of dirt had plowed through the windshield.

"Anoud!"

Quickly he stood and crawled past people to the front of the bus.

"Everyone sit still," the teacher in the back of the bus shouted. "We are all right. Stay in your seats until I can get up front and see who's injured."

Bandar had no idea what the teacher was saying. He was

too busy praying to Allah until he finally reached Anoud.

"Bandar, return to your seat," the teacher shouted.

Bandar heard his name but ignored the rest. Anoud was badly hurt and bleeding. The girl next to her was crying and in shock, but she appeared unharmed. Bandar motioned for her to move so that he could attend to Anoud.

The girl crawled to the floor, but when she saw blood flowing from the bus driver's head she started screaming. Bandar gathered Anoud in his arms and saw Rob come to calm the other girl. Bandar nodded his thanks.

The teacher came forward and issued evacuation orders. He had opened the emergency door in the rear, and the students were filing out of the bus. Bandar paid little attention. He only wanted to hold Anoud close. He closed his eyes and willed his strength to her limp body. She didn't move.

"Bandar, let me have her." Rob had sent the screaming girl toward the exit. The teacher had arrived and was trying to help the driver. Everyone else was out of the bus.

Rob reached for Anoud. "Give her to me. She's bleeding."

Bandar tightened his grip and glared at Rob. He would not let her go.

"We've got to give her first aid, Bandar. She'll bleed to death if you don't let me help her."

Rage filled Bandar. "No male touches my sister." These infidels were mad. He wanted to be at home. He wanted Anoud in the harem where she would be safe. He hated this place. His dear sweet Anoud lay limp and bleeding in his arms.

"Bandar." The teacher had helped the driver out of the bus and had returned for Anoud. "Let go of her and get out of here."

Bandar held tight and glared.

"It's his custom," Rob tried to explain. "No men can touch their women."

"I'm a trained medic, Bandar. She needs help. I can help her."

Bandar started to repeat his refusal to let them touch Anoud. He didn't realize that in his stress he had reverted to his native Arabic.

"Stop that gibberish." Rob lost patience and began to shout. "Give her to the teacher."

He reached for Anoud, but the teacher quickly pulled him away. "I think I can handle this. Go see if you can find a girl who has some first-aid training. Then I can tell her what to do."

Rob was furious, but he finally did as the teacher ordered. Noisily, he stomped out of the bus, cursing the whole way.

Bandar watched him leave with relief. Now if only the infidel teacher would follow.

"Listen, Bandar. He didn't understand your ways. I don't either, but we want to help."

The teacher's tone was low and soothing. "I won't touch her. I can help you though, so you can carry her out."

Bandar relaxed a little.

"Just remember, I don't want to hurt or insult your sister. I want to help her."

The slow speech made sense. Bandar was able to translate now.

"There's help outside, Bandar. There are women doctors who can help Anoud."

Yes, he must get Anoud to a doctor. Slowly he struggled to stand. The teacher reached behind him and, careful not to touch Anoud, steadied his steps.

* * *

Bandar was in a panic because of the accident and his sister's injuries. He wanted to protect her and did what he was used to doing in his culture. He didn't understand that Rob or the teacher could help.

How did patience on the teacher's part serve to help the situation? What were the possible consequences if no one had the insight to be patient with Bandar and explain to him what was going on?

We all panic when we are confronted with danger or what we perceive to be a threatening situation. One of the most effective ways to deal with it is to have patience and understanding.

CHAPTER ◇ 9

Your Attitude Makes A Difference

In previous chapters several scenes have been presented that point out what a difference your attitude makes. Seth's attitude of nonviolence kept him out of trouble. Keesha's attitude of compassion changed the thinking and actions of her fellow students.

We also saw examples of how a negative attitude can cause problems. Julia suffered health problems because of her prejudice and hate. Shelley ended up with financial problems because of her personal lack of security in who she was without what money could buy.

Determination and strength of character are attitudes that carried some of these teens through tough times. Sean and Travis studied and worked to overcome their low-income status. Felipe showed bravery and courage in his action that saved lives.

In all of these events, attitudes determined how they turned out. Positive attitudes led to beneficial events.

Negative attitudes led to unpleasant events. Let's see some other examples that show how this works.

Paul Asuluk and Joe Therchik are Yupik Eskimos who live in a small village in Alaska. They both have teams of dogs for cross-country dogsled treks.

Animals reflect human emotions and attitudes. Being dependent on humans makes them sensitive to their masters' moods. It is the day of the high school–sponsored cross-country dogsled trek. Let's see what kind of moods Joe and Paul are in.

Temperatures ranged below zero, but the cold didn't bother Paul. He had on his sealskin parka and under that a nylon down vest. He didn't worry about the dogs either. Their long, thick fur would keep them plenty warm.

The nylon straps were another matter. The cold had made them stiff, and Paul had difficulty harnessing the dogs.

"Ease up, Bear," he spoke the command gently but firmly to his lead dog. "The strap is almost fastened, so sit still."

Metal clicked as he snapped the harness in place. Wolf bumped into his leg as he wiggled with excitement.

"Save your energy, pup. It's going to be a long trip."

"Which you're never going to finish." A voice Paul recognized interrupted his talk with the dogs.

Reluctantly he looked up to see Joe Therchik, one of his classmates who was signed up for the trek. He greeted him in the traditional Yupik manner, but Joe ignored it and spoke English.

"I don't know why you bother to hitch up. You know my dogs are going to outrun yours."

"We'll see." Paul turned from Joe, embarrassed by his

poor manners. Joe stepped closer and Sheba growled. Paul moved beside her and kept his hand on her neck. The dogs always became restless when Joe was around. Paul suspected it was because of the cruelty Joe used in handling his own dogs.

"The trek is about to begin. You'd better get your team ready," Paul reminded him.

"Don't sweat it. My dogs are always ready."

Paul glanced over to where Joe's sled stood. None of his dogs were lying down as Paul's were. Paul had trained his to conserve energy. Joe's dogs were snarling and nipping at each other.

Just like their master, Paul thought, and then canceled the negative thinking. He needed to concentrate on the event, not on Joe's problems. If he didn't stay calm, his dogs would get restless also.

The trek was about to begin. Paul grasped the back of the sled and glanced around. Behind him, family and friends were gathered to watch the sleds depart. Paul knew they would be preparing for tonight's party while he was fighting the elements in a grueling journey across the ice.

Ahead, snow blew high in the air as the wind whipped past. The crystal flakes shimmered in the glow of the low yellow sun, which never set at this time of year.

"It's all right. Hang in there, fellas. We're going to start soon."

Paul could almost swear that his dogs understood his words, which were murmured in a soothing tone. He knew the dogs were waiting until he gave his high-pitched command. When he did, they'd charge right out of town.

He looked over and saw Joe take a long pull on a bottle of whiskey. A sliver of unease went through Paul. The ice was too dangerous to dull your senses with alcohol. Joe could be trouble.

Joe corked the bottle and then let out a loud howl. His dogs started pacing restlessly within their harness. One dog tripped and Joe snapped the end of a large whip on the dog's nose. His yelp sent chills down Paul's spine.

Paul loved his dogs. He hated to see the way Joe handled his.

Finally the race started, and Paul forgot about Joe. His attention was focused on the thrill of adventure. The sled bounced along the hard-packed ice as the dogs scrambled across the rough terrain.

The sounds of the runners scraping the ice and the yip of dogs brought a wealth of memories. The crisp, cool Arctic air blew against his face. They were on their way.

Everything went smoothly for the first two hours. Paul was ahead of the other four teams. He felt as if he and his dogs were alone in the universe. Maybe someday he'd take his team and travel alone to the North Pole like the Frenchman Jean-Louis Étienne.

Paul remembered reading in *National Geographic* about the explorer's adventure in the Arctic. Paul felt as if he could accomplish anything right now. Perhaps Étienne had felt the same way.

Suddenly a shout carried from across the ice behind him. Surprised, he turned around to see Joe wielding his whip over his head and then cracking it down on the team of dogs.

Paul gritted his teeth as anger began to build. The dogs were straining too much. They could be hurt overdoing like that.

"Ease up," Paul hollered. "Your dogs aren't in shape for this fast pace."

He knew he should have kept his mouth shut, but he couldn't help speaking up for the dogs.

Joe's answer was obscene, and Paul clenched his jaw shut and tried to ignore it.

Joe snapped the whip again. The lead dog yelped. Paul's dogs veered away, losing stride.

"Hey, Therchik. Stay clear of my team," Paul warned.

"If you don't like it, drop back," Joe shouted and let loose with several more curses. He washed them down with another swig from the whiskey bottle.

At that point Paul felt like cursing too, but he didn't. He took deep breaths to stay calm. If he became upset, something he rarely did on a trek, his dogs would react. He didn't need trouble this far out from the village.

Joe snapped his whip again. It crackled over the heads of Paul's team. His dogs veered again, this time sharply enough to tilt the sled. Quick thinking saved him from a spill.

Paul started to shout at Joe but realized it would do no good. In fact, he could tell that Joe was enjoying getting him riled. After a quick glance around, Paul purposely swerved the sled away from Joe. With whistles and commands, he ordered the team to ease off and let Joe pull ahead.

Getting even with Joe was not worth the danger to his team. If Paul didn't contest Joe's position, maybe it would go easier for Joe's dogs also. Paul looked at their tired bodies and felt a wave of pity. Joe didn't exercise them enough. This sudden burst of unaccustomed exertion was taking its toll.

Joe widened the gap between himself and Paul. Relief began to settle over Paul with the return of his earlier peace. He saw that his dogs were running more smoothly now and more as a team.

His peace didn't last long. A terrible crunching noise

came from ahead. Joe screamed, and dogs howled as the sled rolled over.

Paul hurried toward the accident. By the time he got there Joe's dogs were a tangled mess, snarling and biting at each other. None appeared hurt.

Joe was another matter. When Paul's team came even with the overturned sled, he saw that Joe was pinned underneath. Quickly, he commanded his dogs to halt and ran over to Joe.

"How bad is it?" he asked.

Joe rolled his eyes and tried to talk, but all that came out was a drunken slur. Disgusted, Paul glanced up in time to see the other teams approaching. He signaled for them to stop.

While the others lifted the sled off of Joe and put him on one of their sleds, Paul worked to settle Joe's dogs down. They snarled and growled, but Paul ignored it. He continued a steady flow of soothing words as he tried to unhook the harnesses and get the dogs away from the sled.

"We've got Joe," one of the men hollered.

"How bad is he?"

"Lucky son-of-a-gun doesn't appear to have more than a slight concussion."

"Must be all the booze he's been guzzling."

"Our luck, too," someone muttered. "There goes the trek. By the time we get Joe and his dogs back the day will be shot."

Several more grumbles filled the air as they strapped Joe onto one of the sleds.

Paul, still holding onto Joe's dogs, said, "You guys go on back with Joe. I'll bring his dogs along as soon as I settle them down."

No one argued that decision. Most of them were afraid of Joe's dogs. Paul wasn't because he knew that as soon as Joe and the other angry and upset people were gone, the dogs would settle down.

Sure enough, when the last team disappeared over the horizon, the dogs quieted and let Paul handle them.

Joe's negative attitudes, his cruelty, and his sharpness caused turmoil around him. His dogs were irritable. How did Paul feel when Joe was around?

Our effect on others becomes more obvious with animals because they don't have the mechanisms to hide their feelings. In the same way that Joe's attitude affected the dogs, it affected people he came in contact with.

Think about people you know who are always complaining; mad at something, someone, or some group; talking maliciously about others; or putting people down. How do you feel after you've been around someone like that?

Soon you will find that you are upset, that you are complaining, that you are putting people down. This outer turmoil causes inner stress as well. You begin to feel nervous and uptight. It is possible that you'll do as Joe did and find alcohol or drugs to settle the unrest.

The real solution is simple. You need to change your attitude. Paul's calm nature settled Joe's dogs as soon as Joe (the negative influence) was gone.

How did Paul handle stressful incidents? What was his attitude toward his dogs and toward others? How does that generate a positive attitude?

Evaluate your life-style and see if there are any negative elements you can get rid of. You will be surprised how it can change your life. Instead of unrest and turmoil, you will have inner peace, strength, and a happier outlook on life.

Having a happy attitude may seem out of reach for you.

It would seem easy for people to be content if they had money, for example, or if they had a carefree life with no work. It isn't the outer circumstances that cause inner peace. Let's look at Doug, Kono, Chin, and Manuel, four friends who are surfing at Sunset Beach in Hawaii.

"Look at those waves?" Kono shook his dark head. "They're building up fast."

Doug glanced from his Hawaiian friend back to the water. "Give 'em another half hour and they'll be perfect for surfing," Doug agreed as he brushed back his blond hair. "What do you think, Chin?"

"For sure," Chin agreed. "We're gonna hang ten today."

Manuel cast a questioning glance, and quickly Doug explained the beach conditions. Manuel had come from the Philippines just a month ago. He didn't know much about local conditions yet, but he sure could surf.

Manuel shifted in the sand. "When are we going out?"

"Save your energy. We'll wait till it gets good," Chin advised.

"You always want perfection," Kono teased. "You won't settle for less."

"And why should I? When there's a choice between perfect and average, which are you going to choose?"

"I'm not like you," Kono said, suddenly bitter. "I don't get the choices that you have."

Everyone fell silent at that. The four friends were all well aware that away from this beach they lived in different worlds. Chin's father was one of the richest merchants on the island. Kono's family owned a pineapple plantation and so had a sizable income, but a large family and hard labor cut into the profits. Doug's parents were relatively poor, living on the salary of a Chief Petty Officer in the Navy. Manuel, a recent immigrant, had nothing.

"Come off it," Doug rounded on Kono. "You're one to talk about privilege. You've got it made, yet all you ever do is complain."

"You don't have to work hours after school like I do. You get to lie around on the beach and look at all the pretty *wahine* girls."

Doug laughed at that. "Yeah! Life is a real dog, Kono. You don't have to study your tail off to qualify for a scholarship. You don't have to worry about going to some dumb university on the mainland. You've got it made right here."

"No way." Kono shook his head. "I'll trade places with you any day. You come work at my place from sunup to sundown and see how good that university is going to look."

"I don't know what you guys are complaining about," Manuel said when he finally got a chance. "I'd give anything to have a job, let alone worry if it was all day or not."

"You've got a point," Doug rubbed his neck. "Whatever you don't have, you always want."

Chin shifted forward. "Then you should go get it. I have to work long hours too for my father. Do you think he just gave me that car?"

All four turned to stare at the red sports car and nodded their heads.

"No way," Chin told them. "I wanted that car, and I had to work for it. Only I got smart. I looked around and decided what job *I* wanted to do. Then I went and asked Father before he gave me one I didn't want."

"You sly fox," Doug slapped his bare knee. "I bet he thought you were a real go-getter."

Chin smiled. "You bet. I number one son." He imitated

the old Charlie Chan character. "But I work like number one slave. My father doesn't know the word play."

Doug stared out at the sunlight sparkling on the waves. He *was* lucky, he guessed. He just never stopped to think about it. There were always too many things he didn't have or couldn't do. All his energy had been wasted on thinking about those things instead of what he could do.

"Come on, guys. Lets go out and do what I do best. Surf's up and I'm in."

No one needed further urging. Muscles bulged as they lifted their boards. Tan skin glistened in the bright sun. The breeze tossed their hair as the strode into the perfect Hawaiian surf.

Chin and Kono had material advantages. Doug and Manuel had time to spend at the beach. Seemingly these four should be happy and satisfied with their lives. Would you be, in their places? Why are some of them not content?

Think of each one and determin way he could change his attitude into a more positive one. If they don't do so, they are going to live on one of the most beautiful places in the world and not even realize how fortunate they are.

Can you see how material conditions and outer circumstances do not bring contentment and peace? Positive attitudes begin within.

Let's look at Gloria, Juanita, Sabrina, and Carolyn. They live in a town on the U.S./Mexico border. Outwardly they do not have much. Their families are relatively poor. Let's see if that has affected their lives in a negative or a positive manner.

* * *

It was sunny in Juanita's backyard but not quite warm. The December air had a slight chill that the girls hoped would burn off as the day wore on. They had a lot of work to do.

"Brrr." Gloria shivered as she carried a pot of *masa* and put it on the large table Uncle Pedro had set up for the girls. "Too bad we can't make these tamales inside."

"It's warm in there now, but if we were all in that small room and cooking. . . why, girl, we would cook too," Gloria said as she tossed over the packages of corn husks. "It'll warm up in no time."

"We're going to be so busy," Carolyn predicted. "I'm dying to know how to put together these tamales. Your Mom makes the best in town."

"That's right." Sabrina came up behind the girls and held out the wooden spoons and spatulas that Juanita's mother had given her. Ma says to be sure to bring some home."

"You'll get some," Juanita promised. "Everyone who helps takes a couple dozen home."

"Yum." Sabrina rubbed her stomach. "Let's get to work."

It didn't take long for Gloria to show Sabrina and Carolyn how to spread the *masa* on the corn husk. Juanita was in charge of putting in the meat and olives. Gloria would wrap them up. By ten-thirty they had it down to a routine and had forgotten the chill in the air.

Laughter echoed around the yard as the girls talked. Gloria's cousin Julio had come by and turned on some music. If the girls weren't talking, they were singing.

By eleven the sounds from the yard were getting louder.

"What's going on here? What's all this racket?" Julio strolled into the yard, a wrench in his hand from the work he'd been doing on his car. He winked at Sabrina, and when she lowered her head to blush, he reached around her to snatch an olive and pop it in his mouth.

"*Ratón*," Juanita slapped his fingers with a spatula. "You leave those alone or you won't get any tamales for Christmas dinner."

He turned big brown eyes toward Sabrina. "You wouldn't be so cruel, would you?"

Sabrina laughed. "Get on with you, boy. You can't give me no puppy-dog look and think I'm going to give in."

He wiggled his eyebrows up and down. "I was hoping." He grinned as he left the yard and returned to the garage.

All four girls started giggling.

"Julio is flirting with you, Sabrina."

"No way." Sabrina started smoothing the *masa* back and forth on the husk.

"He better not," Carolyn stated. "Pa would have a fit."

"Why? 'Cause he's not black?" Juanita teased.

Sabrina handed her the husk and shook her head. "He'd have a fit if a black boy flirted."

"It don't matter, black, or Mexican, or even white." Carolyn chuckled. "He doesn't want *any* boys looking at Sabrina."

"Oh, oh. You're going to have fun on dates," Gloria sympathized.

"I can just picture it," Carolyn said as she handed more husks to Juanita. "Your Dad will be standing there like a football player. No guy's going to dare set foot inside your door."

"Don't worry," Sabrina sent them a mischievous grin. "I can handle Pa."

"What about your folks, Juanita?" Carolyn asked. "What are they saying about your dates with Rafael?"

Juanita blushed, and all the girls chuckled. They loved to tease her, so she'd have to be careful how she answered.

"She went out with him last night," Gloria told them.

"Big mouth," Juanita scolded. She was in for it now. They would want to know everything. "We just went to the movies. I'll be back. We need more olives."

In a flash she hurried into the kitchen. Maybe they'd think of something else to talk about. When she returned to the yard, she knew her ploy hadn't worked. All three were standing there, obviously ready to hear everything.

These girls do not have material wealth, they are from different cultures and races, and they even speak different languages, yet there was no conflict during their interaction. Juanita and Gloria were showing Sabrina and Carolyn how to make the tamales that are traditionally served at Christmas in Mexican families. No big issue was made of the different ways the holiday is celebrated.

Julio came into the yard and flirted with Sabrina. The issue of race was mentioned, but no one took offense at it. Spanish was spoken, but in a way that didn't leave a non-speaker out. The meaning was quite clear.

The absence of wealth didn't even enter into the conversation. These girls didn't have much money, yet they seemed happy.

Attitude is the determining factor. If Sabrina had taken offense at Julio's flirting or if she had been insulted by the discussion, conflict would have occurred. Sabrina decided how she would react.

Juanita and Gloria didn't have to invite Carolyn and Sabrina over to make tamales. The girls didn't have to come. They had open and accepting minds and gained by sharing cultural knowledge.

Your life is determined by your attitude toward it. You make the choice and decide if you will have a life filled with bitterness, malice, hatred, jealousy, and anger or one filled with kindness, self-control, happiness, and sharing.

You may not feel that you have control of the physical world around you or the situations you have to deal with, but you do have the power to decide how you personally are going to react. It is your life. No one else can live it for you. No one can change it but you.

In the next chapter, we will see how your attitude affects others.

CHAPTER ◇ 10

What Goes Around Comes Around

In the last chapter we discussed how you can control your attitude and your reactions to your physical world. Sometimes the physical events and conditions that surround you seem out of your control. You cannot determine the reactions of other people. They have the same free will that you do. You can, however, have an influence on how you are treated.

How you decide to react can influence others or affect the situation. Remember Keesha and the soccer game? Her act of kindness influenced Teresa. She set an example for others to follow. Keesha didn't force Teresa to help Barbara. She simply showed the team players that kindness was an option. They might not have thought so, considering Margarita's behavior.

We can influence others in a positive manner as Keesha did, or we can influence them in a negative manner as Margarita did. However we decide to react, our actions affect others. Because of that, our behavior usually comes full circle and determines how people treat us.

Remember Danny at the shopping mall? Mr. Stewart treated Danny with compassion and understanding. His reaction affected Danny in a positive manner by changing Danny's opinions about blacks. The next time Danny sees a black he will be more considerate. His friendly attitude will be healthier for him than his previous antagonistic attitude.

Antagonistic behavior usually causes fights. Danny's friendly behavior will cause nothing less than a friendly nod. Can you see how it works to come full circle?

Take for another example a girl who gossips. She always manages to dig up the latest dirt on everybody. Other teens flock to her to hear the latest, but are their feelings toward her filled with trust? When you've been around someone like that don't you wonder what she's saying about you?

The fact that we do wonder leads us to ask questions and find out things about her. The gossiping goes full circle. She talks maliciously about others. They talk maliciously about her.

What if this hypothetical girl always had something good to say about everybody? What would people say about a teen like her?

In this last chapter we're going to a concert by a popular rock band; we'll examine how our attitudes affect others and come back to affect us.

The light finally turned green. Stuart pressed the gas pedal and shifted gears. His red Corvette shot across the intersection. Ahead he saw signs for the coliseum. Good. They didn't have time for getting lost. The concert was to start in less than an hour.

Stuart glanced at Heather, who had pulled the visor down so she could see in the mirror.

"You look great," Stuart told her.

Her long blonde hair shimmered in the sunlight as she ran a comb through it.

"We aren't going to be late, are we?" She pouted, and Stuart wished he could lean over and give her a kiss.

"No way, babe. Didn't I say I'd get you there?"

She smiled and Stuart took a deep breath. He'd been wanting to date her for months. Now that she wasn't going with Mr. Football anymore, he'd finally been able to ask her out. The concert's timing had been perfect. Heather loved this particular band.

At the entrance, traffic police were directing the cars toward the far end of the lot where there were still parking spaces. They seemed at least a mile from the huge structure. He glanced at Heather's high heels and thought about his styled hair that would get messed up in the wind. No way was he going to walk that distance.

"Hang on," he said as he swerved to the left when the policeman wasn't looking.

Heather gasped, "Where are you going?"

"This way. We'll find a place up here closer to the stadium."

"How? They'll be filled, won't they?"

"Trust me. I know what I'm doing." He shifted gears. His tires squeaked as he swerved down a row. "See up ahead? They count so many cars for each section. Not everyone is actually parked yet."

"But you're going the wrong way." She grasped the dash and held on.

"Calm down." He wished she'd shut up. Didn't she think he knew what he was doing?

Ahead of him, cars were pulling into parking places. If he was fast, he could squeeze in front of one before it actually got in.

Stuart downshifted and prepared to make his move. Heather gasped, but he ignored her. Carefully he watched the other cars. A Cutlass slid into place, a Thunderbird followed. Next a beat-up pickup shifted into gear. Its engine sputtered. Stuart saw his chance and slipped into the truck's spot.

"Stuart! You can't do that."

"I just did." He chuckled in triumph. "Come on. If we hurry we'll be in time."

"But what if that guy is mad? I'd sure be angry," Heather said.

Stuart was starting to get mad himself. "Forget it. Ready? Are you coming or not?"

Before Heather could answer, a loud thud sounded on the rear of his car. Stuart jumped out.

"This is my spot, buddy." A guy stood by the rear fender of his car.

A quick glance at the open door of the truck showed where he'd come from. Two other guys, obviously friends of this wacko, stood beside the truck.

Stuart eyed the worn jeans, tennis shoes with holes, and T-shirt. This jerk was no match for him.

"I got here first." Stuart shrugged. "That's the breaks."

"We'll see about the breaks," the guy said. "How about if I break your neck?"

Before he could react, Stuart was attacked. As soon as the guy planted his fist in Stuart's stomach, the other two joined him. All was blackness as Stuart lost consciousness.

* * *

Think about Stuart's attitude and how it got him into trouble. He treated others with disrespect, and they returned the treatment. Stuart thought that because of his wealth he should be afforded special privilege. In fact, that attitude may very well have worked for him before.

The three in the truck could have given in to Stuart's bullying tactics. They might have complained, sworn at him, or simply let the matter drop. Stuart's behavior, though, was to provoke the wrong person. What he dished out, he received, and not necessarily in equal proportion.

What are some other alternatives to the situation, and how would you have handled the matter if you had been the driver of the truck? Would you have sought revenge as he did, or would you have reported to the police or let the matter go? There is a saying, "What goes around comes around."

Ernesto and Joaquín are at the concert that Stuart was trying to get to. They, however, are already inside and seated in the balcony. They have good seats for seeing the show, but they are still not happy. Let's see why.

"*Ese.* I don't want to sit here," Joaquín spoke in Spanish so the two girls sitting next to him wouldn't understand.

"Why?" Ernesto reverted to Spanish also. "We can see really well from here."

"It's them." Joaquín pointed to the black girls. "I hate the smell of that junk they put on their hair."

Just then a blonde and brunette sat on the other side of Ernesto. They were gorgeous.

"You have all the luck, *amigo.*"

"That's for sure," Ernesto replied. "I'm going to like sitting here."

"No," Joaquín groaned. "Let's go see if we can switch."

"With who? No one's going to move now."

Joaquín knew his friend was right. He took a deep breath and almost gagged.

Ernesto sighed. "Here, *amigo*. If it's that bad, you trade places with me."

Joaquín felt like a heel, but only for a moment. He really hated that junk. For several minutes they debated about whether to trade or not. Their Spanish blended into the noise around them. Finally Joaquín agreed. They switched places.

Ernesto smiled at the two black girls before he sat down. Good old Ernesto, always nice to everyone. It made him laugh. Or maybe it made him feel a bit guilty. No. Joaquín shrugged off the thought. Those girls meant nothing to him.

Now these two on his right, they were something else. Ernesto was crazy to give up his seat next to them.

Joaquín was about to send them the smile that charmed most girls, but they stood up and headed toward the concessions.

"Tough luck," Ernesto teased.

"They'll be back." Joaquín wasn't worried. He was good-looking, and he knew it. Girls were always flirting with him. He'd be doing those two a favor even to talk to them.

Crowds poured into the stadium. Joaquín and Ernesto looked for friends but saw only a couple in the mass of people.

"This concert is going to be the best," Ernesto grinned.

Joaquín laughed. "You enjoy everything, *amigo*. To you, everything is the best."

Shaking his head, Joaquín thought about that for a few minutes. Must be nice to see things from Ernesto's point of view. Joaquín tried, but he was too much of a realist. Besides, he didn't have Ernesto's trust in people. You always had to watch out for the other guy. He could stab you in the back, and then what would all your trust and good intentions get you? No, it was better to be prepared.

The stadium was almost filled when the blonde and brunette returned to their seats. The blonde sat next to him. Joaquín resisted the urge to brush back his hair and straighten his shirt. *You look great*, he told himself. He nudged Ernesto and gave him the signal to watch this. It was time to make his move.

He fixed on his face the smile that the girls all loved and turned to the girl next to him. His pose was casual.

"Good seats." He nodded toward the stage.

The girl looked at him with a blank expression. Joaquín shifted. It was noisy in here with the crowd still moving about and talking.

He leaned closer. "I said we have good seats."

The blonde backed away as if he'd said something obscene.

"Hey! What..."

She interrupted. "I'm sorry, but I don't speak Spanish."

Surprised, Joaquín sat back. Beside him, Ernesto began to laugh.

"Serves you right, *amigo*."

Joaquín looked past him at the black girls. They were chuckling too. Angry and slightly ashamed, he faced the stage.

Joaquín basically received the same treatment from the blonde that he'd given the black girls. Discrimination is not exclusive to one race. Every human being has stereotyped views of others and has personal likes and dislikes.

How you treat others usually reflects back to you. It is

possible that the blonde had noticed how Joaquín acted toward the other girls. If she did, it was bound to influence how she felt about Joaquín and how she treated him.

We may not actually verbalize our feelings, but we project our attitudes. One way this occurs is through body language. Have you ever met someone and without his saying a word you know he doesn't want to talk to you? Perhaps the person obviously turns away or just turns slightly. His face becomes blank instead of having a welcoming expression. It becomes clear that he doesn't want you around.

Another way we let people know our attitude is by our thought waves. Most people don't realize how we affect others by our thoughts. They are projected like sound waves and are received by those around us.

Take for example a room with two people in it. You walk in, and no one is speaking. They aren't even moving. Yet you know that those two people were arguing before you entered the room. You can feel their anger and sense the tension. Thought waves of anger are transmitted, and you receive the message loud and clear.

Think back to other incidents. You probably recall times when you knew you had interrupted an intimate conversation or that the people in the room had been laughing. Sometimes you sense that someone is sad or in pain. Those feelings occur because you received the thought waves.

This process is how you generate people's attitude toward you. If your thoughts are full of hatred, you will put people around you in a defensive mood. That will create an antagonistic atmosphere.

Conversely, if your thoughts are full of patience, kindness, and positive attitudes, people around you will not feel threatened. They will open up and be relaxed enough to be friendly.

Not only do your thoughts create positive behavior, but so do your actions. If you are generous, kind, and friendly to others, in all likelihood people will be gentle, friendly, and kind to you. Lets look at Chris, Ted, Jenny, and Tracy. They are friends from the same middle-class neighborhood and have also come to the concert.

"I can't believe I'm sitting here." Jenny sat back and looked around the huge stadium.

"You wouldn't want to miss this," Tracy smiled. "It's your favorite band. We know that."

Chris, Tracy's boyfriend, leaned forward so he could be heard. "You only go crazy every time one of their songs comes on."

"I do not." Jenny pretended to be indignant but was too happy to make a pouty expression.

Ted, who was sitting on her other side, put his arm around her shoulders and squeezed. "You can't fool us. We know you too well."

That was certainly true, Jenny thought. They'd all been friends since grade school. It was the only reason she had let them chip in and pay for her ticket. They understood about the money problems her family was having. Ever since her father had been in the car accident and unable to work, her family had been struggling to make ends meet.

"I am excited," she admitted. "I've wanted to see this group for ages."

Her friends spoke in chorus. "We know."

Jenny laughed. She had every album the band had recorded, every poster, and a copy of every article written about them.

T-shirts with their picture were being sold out front. She'd love to have one of those too but didn't dare mention it. Her friends would buy one for her. She had some measure of pride.

"Don't you give me a bad time," she scolded. "You like this group too."

"Only because you cram them down our throats," Chris teased.

"Yeah. They're the only thing we get to listen to around you."

For several more minutes Jenny kidded around with her friends. But when the lights blinked the warning for people to settle in their seats, a large lump formed in her throat. For a second she thought she might cry, but she quickly swallowed back the tears.

Tracy and Ted must have sensed her emotional state, because they reached for her hands and held them tight.

She smiled at them. "You guys are the greatest to bring me here. I don't deserve friends like you."

"Yes, you do. You're always doing stuff for us," Tracy told her.

"No, I'm not. I just. . ."

"What about how you baby-sat my sister so that I could go to that party at Chris's church?"

"That was nothing. Your folks couldn't help it if they had to go to that office party at the last minute. I don't mind watching little Michelle."

"And how about the other day when you came over and helped me with the yard so I could go to band practice?" Ted reminded her.

"That practice was unexpected. You didn't have a chance to plan ahead."

Chris leaned forward. "Remember last week when you ran those errands for me? Man, I thought my parents were going to kill me."

Jenny blushed, embarrassed about all the fuss over everyday things. "Come on, you guys. You're my friends. What do you expect?"

"You're always sacrificing to do stuff for others, Jenny. You deserve this treat," Ted said.

Chris chimed in. "And it's about time we got to be the ones to do something for you."

Ted hugged Jenny's shoulders. "We're lucky this concert was coming to town so we'd have a way to do something special for you."

Jenny leaned her head on Ted's shoulder to hide the tears welling up in her eyes. Her friends would think she was nuts to be crying like this, but they made her so happy.

This incident is an exaggerated example of the rewards of kindness, but it isn't impossible. Jenny was a thoughtful and caring person. Her family had financial problems, so she couldn't share in a material way. It didn't matter. She gave of her time and energy. She helped her friends in their individual cases of need.

Because her actions were generous, her friends were inspired to repay her kindness by their own generosity. Their gift was her ticket to the concert.

In these three examples you can see that your behavior and attitude determine how people treat you. Now you need to decide how you want to live.

Are you interested in a peaceful existence or one filled with turmoil? You make the choice by thinking negative or positive thoughts.

Because of that, your thoughts determine how your interaction with others will go. In dealing with multicultural people, you need to keep your mind open and caring if you want successful relationships.

We have seen how many different relationships are involved with multicultural interaction. The obvious differences are because people are from different countries and speak other languages, but there are also varieties of cultures within the United States.

Some of the cultures are regional, some racial, and some are religious in nature. Subtle differences exist in socio-economic class levels. These are not as obvious, but they are just as real.

The United States guarantees religious freedom and equal opportunities for every person within our boundaries. How we respond to that right is up to each of us.

If you harbor prejudice, hatred, or intolerance, it is probable that contact will be an unpleasant experience. If you practice patience, kindness, and generosity, there is every reason to expect a pleasant interaction.

The important fact to remember is that whatever the circumstance, it is your choice that determines the outcome. You choose your thoughts. You choose your actions. Your thoughts and actions determine how people react to you.

Recommended Reading

Fiction

Arrick, Fran. *Chernowitz!* Scarsdale, NY: Bradbury Press, 1981.

Jones, Toeckey. *Skin Deep.* New York: Harper & Row Publishers, 1986.

Lee, Harper. *To Kill a Mockingbird.* Philadelphia & New York: J.B. Lippincott Co., 1960.

Rhue, Morton. *The Wave.* New York: Delacorte Press, 1981.

Ruby, Lois. *Two Truths in My Pocket.* New York: Viking Press, 1982.

Sebestyen, Ouida. *Words by Heart.* Boston & Toronto: Little, Brown & Co., 1979.

Yep, Laurence. *Dragonwings.* New York: Harper & Row, 1975.

Nonfiction

Alexander, Rae. *Young and Black in America.* New York: Random House, 1970.

Arnold, Caroline. *Anti-Semitism.* New York: Julian Messner, 1986.

Froman, Robert. *Racism.* New York: Delacorte Press, 1972.

Gomez, David F. *Somos Chicanos: Strangers in Our Own Land.* Boston: Beacon Press, 1973.

Griffin, John Howard. *A Time to Be Human,* New York: Macmillan. 1977.

McFarland, Rhoda. *Coping Through Self-Esteem,* New York: Rosen Publishing Group, 1988.

———. *Coping with Stigma.* New York: Rosen Publishing Group, 1989.

Meltzer, Milton. *The Human Rights Book.* New York: Farrar, Straus, Giroux, 1981.

Sung, Betty Lee. *The Chinese in America*, New York: Macmillan, 1972.

Index

A
acceptance, into upper class, 45
alcohol, 121
Amish, 34, 39–42, 72, 87
anger, 42, 78, 82, 85, 118, 128, 136
Arabic, 113
attitude
  disrespectful, 133
  gentle, 70
  harmful, 77–78
  importance of, 115–128
  improving, 24
  intolerant, 42
  negative, 86, 115–116, 121, 129
  positive, 27, 115, 121, 124, 129, 136
  understanding, 65, 130

B
behavior
  alternatives of, 65
  antagonistic, 130
  culturally accepted, 45, 46
  prejudicial, 65, 69–70, 77, 82
  religious, 39
  violent, 42, 72
bilingualism, 2–3, 20, 31–32
blacks, 21, 25, 59, 61–65, 66–69, 73–76, 87, 126–127, 130, 133
  prejudice against, 69, 71
body language, 90, 136
border community, 20–21, 124–128
Buddhism, 42

C
career, choosing, 1–2
Catholics, 34–38, 42
change, adjustment to, 2–3
Chicanos, 65, 69
classes
  economic, 44–57
  social, 3
communication, language as, 18–19, 20, 24
compassion, 16, 70, 77, 86, 100, 101, 115, 130
conflict, of cultures, 91–96
courage, 2, 100, 115
cults, religious, 72
culture, 1, 3, 101
  Navajo, 28–31
  religion as part of, 2
customs, religious, 39, 113

D
differences
  cultural, 5–17, 70, 71, 84,

96–100, 105
language, 3
racial, 3, 70, 71
religious, 33–43, 71
Dineh, 20
drugs, 59–60, 64, 121

E
economic ladder, 44, 46, 50, 57
education, 2
and class system, 45–46
embarrassment, 9, 11, 15, 38, 56, 80, 96
empathy, 15, 25
English
as dominant language, 20–21
as first language, 6
as foreign language, 10–13, 80
as second language, 19, 25, 104–105
envy, 52, 71–85, 86
ethics, 39, 42

F
faiths, different, 33–43
fear, 71–85
of change, 2
in foreign school, 14, 23–25
of minorities, 66–69
of what others think, 15, 16–17
feelings, 101
consideration for others', 57
negative, 28, 82
freedom, religious, 1, 2, 3, 33, 43, 140
frustration, 23

G
gangs, 59, 64
generosity, 56, 137, 139–140
geographical differences, 5–6
gossip, 130

H
harassment
of Amish, 41, 72
of middle-class students, 50
Hare Krishna, 34
hate cults, 72
hatred, 62, 71–72, 75, 76, 81, 85, 86, 128, 136, 140
hinduism, 42
Hispanics, 21

I
immigrants, 1, 7, 20, 33
Mexican, 7–14, 16
India, 59, 102–105
influence, on others, 129–130
insecurity, 27, 42
Islam, 42

J
Japan, 105–110
jealousy, 76–77, 128
Jews, 37–38, 39, 42, 82–84
Hasidic, 34

K
kindness, acts of, 16, 65, 77, 85, 86–100, 101, 110, 128, 129, 136, 137, 139–140

L
language, 1, 2
as communication, 27
different, 18–32, 72, 101
national, 6, 19
second, 8, 17, 18, 24, 105
Lebanon, 21–23
life-style
evaluating, 121–122
varying, 3, 5–6

M
mental telepathy, 31
Mexican Americans, 72–76, 124–126
Mexicans, 80–81, 124–126, 127
mobility, class, 44–46
multilingualism, 20
Muslims, 21–23, 110–115

N
Native American, 21, 59
Native American Church, 43
Navajo, 6, 20, 29, 43
need, to learn language, 19, 20–21, 24
nonviolence, 39–42, 87, 115

O
Old World, 94
opinion, informed, 58

P
patience, 21, 32, 101–113, 136, 140
peers
impressing, 42
pressure from, 53, 109
poverty, 51, 53, 57, 139
prejudice, 42, 58–70, 72, 81, 110, 140
pride, hurt, 57, 67
Protestants, 27–28, 42

R
race, 3, 60–65
reaction
negative, 15, 71, 84, 86
positive, 17
regional differences, 5–6
religion, 1, 33–43
freedom of, 2, 3
prejudice in, 70
revenge, 65, 71, 84, 87, 133

S
Saudi Arabia, 110–114
school
attending foreign, 14, 20
choosing, 2
exchange programs, 7
secrets, in foreign language, 27
segregation, religious, 33–34
self-confidence, 16, 17
self-hatred, 42
self-image, 71–72
Seventh Day Adventists, 39
Spanish, 19, 21, 25–26, 27, 79–80, 133–135
stereotyping, racial, 64–65, 69–70, 135
stress, 113, 121
students
immigrants, 7–14, 101–114
Hispanic, 19
variety of, 3–4

T
thought waves, 136
tolerance, 2, 24, 27, 33
traditions, preserving, 2

U
ulcer, 80–81, 82, 85

V
values, 3, 39, 42
Vietnamese, 1, 25–26, 27, 87–90
violence, 71, 72

W
whites, 21, 72–76, 126
  prejudice against, 76–77
  prejudice by, 69